CRYING SHAME

by

Sharon Braxton

Crying Shame
by Sharon Braxton

Visit the Web site at: *www.cryingshame.org*

International Standard Book Number: 0-9762600-0-X
Library of Congress Catalog Number: 2005900766

10 9 8 7 6 5 4 3 2 1
First Edition

This book is a work of fiction. Names, characters, places, and incidents are either the product of the author's imagination or are used fictitiously. Any resemblance to actual events or locales or persons, living or dead, is entirely coincidental.

Printed in the United States of America

PATIENCE

I started my novel as a short story at Columbia University in NYC. I remember the weekend I decided to write. It was spring of 1999. It was Memorial Weekend to be exact. One of my closest friends from Maryland wanted to come to NYC to hang out. My plans were to stay in and complete my book B.T.E.O.T.W. (by the end of the weekend)! I made it to Sunday, completing 70 pages and was totally burnt out from writing! What was I thinking? I had a burning desire to hit the streets with my girlfriends. We headed to my friend, Mr. T. Lover's buddies house in Long Island for a cookout. Shortly after that weekend, the course ended and so did my focus on writing! My passion was more on my marketing career in the entertainment industry.

In the summer of 2000 I received an incredible job offer in entertainment in Massachusetts. I kept my place in New York and traveled back and forth from Newton, Massachusetts on the weekends to hang out. That winter I had the opportunity to participate in a Harvard Writer's course for First Time Authors. The student had to be in the fourth chapter of their novel. I soon discovered it was true what they said about attending Harvard! I had never been in a classroom with so many brilliant students in my life. It was the most incredible educational experience I had ever had, with the exception of the Landmark Forum.

Shortly after I completed the course and my novel, I decided I needed to be in a warmer climate! I left Boston on another career path, same industry! I happened to be talking to a potential client one day and shared that I had written a novel. He and his contacts became angels to me. He put me in contact with his agent, a senior level executive at a highly respected publishing company, and a self-publisher who had done very well. He told me to make my final decision after I had spoken to the people aforementioned. I would like to share with you a few things I learned during this entire writing process:

1. If it is too easy, chances are you will not appreciate it. Patience can be a skill or an acquired behavior, whichever one, know that it is required in life to be the best you can be.

2. No one can do you like you do you!

3. Figure out your purpose in life and soar my friends soar....

Thank you all for reading my novel. It is much appreciated.

ACKNOWLEGEMENTS

I would like to first thank GOD for giving me the talent and drive to write this book and the character to *eventually* become patient and stay focused.

Thank you mom (Regina Jamison) for reading my book in its infancy and providing me with your valuable input as well as giving me your honest feedback. Thanks for being my rock always!

Thank you, Aaron (Kiki), my brother for all of your advice throughout this long and difficult process. I guess I am following in your footsteps again. I'm blessed to have a brother like you. You're amazing.

To my Godparents, Joe and Ann Pitts, thanks for supporting and celebrating all of my accomplishments, no matter how large or small.

To my beautiful cousins - Towanda and Trina Braxton, thanks for your fashion contributions. You really know your high-end shoes! You ladies are blessed to have toured around the world with your singing career. I am proud to be a part of such a talented family.

To my mentor, Carl McCaskill, one of the most brilliant men I know, thanks for giving me constructive criticism on my manuscript and providing me with your endless advice and marketing ideas. Thanks for keeping me grounded. Of course - behind every good man is a great woman - Betty McCaskill, thanks for your kindness.

To my Northeastern University (undergrad) friend, Raynelle Swilling - Thanks for taking time out of your busy writing schedule to assist me in my crazy quests for editors. Thanks for always having a calm spirit in the midst of my multiple blizzard-like storms to finish this book!

To my Editors - Kathy Murav - Thanks for taking time out of your Universal Studios schedule to reshape my book. Monica Harris, one of the most well respected African American Editors in NYC, thank you for your expertise. Teri Clemons - One of my fabulous Aunts! Thank you for the line edits.

To David Malki, thank you for your brilliant suggestions and dedication to *Crying Shame*. Thanks for fully understanding my direction and bringing my vision to the cover. You rock!

To the Pilots of American Airlines and AmericaWest - Thanks for your input on jets!

To Professor Holinger and my Harvard classmates - thanks for your raw honesty! It truly made me a better storyteller.

In memory of my Dad, Jasper Braxton, may his strength of a lion and integrity of honor always remain within me.

CHAPTER 1
GOOD BYE
BIANCA

Hello Mr. Ricky Jamal Simmons,

I apologize for emailing you, as opposed to having this conversation face to face. But I really have to say this now before I discard your email address and the horrible memory of you and your wicked ways. You are truly an immature idiot. What kind of man conducts himself in the manner that you have? Don't answer back. I reiterate. I'm trying to put our relationship behind me but I guess in life when one makes such a harsh mistake, it eats at you. At the end of the day, the only person looking back at you in the mirror, is you. I realize you need therapy, but I'm not getting paid to provide it for you.

In the future, don't mislead people. It's not cool. It is obvious that you missed out on getting some pertinent information while growing up, i.e., HOW TO COMMUNICATE WITH A WOMAN and how to feel comfortable in your own skin!

What was the point of lying? Being with me, I thought I would have made you become a better man.

The old saying of, "be careful what you wish for," keep flashing in my mind. People our age are moving forward in their careers, getting married, traveling and enjoying life. The next time you find yourself in a so-called relationship, try being the man you say you are. It would be less costly, in time, money, and headache for all involved. Don't worry, this is the last email. Don't bother replying, my computer has been programmed to reject all incoming messages from you. Next time you meet the RIGHT woman – make sure you've figured out how NOT to be the WRONG man.

God forgives but life does not. Now you can erase....

Bianca Baxter clicked 'send' on her computer and away went the goodbye letter to her on-and-off again boyfriend Ricky Simmons.

She sighed and took a deep breath as she thought about her life and her last night's performance. Bianca, America's Balladeer Beauty rocked the house last night with a high-energy performance which received rave reviews in all of New York's morning papers.

Everyone in her crew, from the band to the dancers wore white in the performance. As the lights simmered she walked down the aisle where the audience was located like the humans dressed in animal costumes in the mega Broadway hit, The Lion King. Her dancers entered onto the stage and did the most amazing dance routine the critics had ever witnessed. The crowd was ooing and aahing. Bianca appeared in a sexy red and white Miu Miu ensemble, consisting of a red and white halter top, white hip hugger pants, and Marc Jacob white leather pointed toed boots, with a four-inch heel. The stage opened and Bianca appeared elegantly gliding along in an oversized old school red wagon, pulled by a gorgeous, muscular man, while she sang the first verse of her platinum single, FUN.

"REMEMBER THE DAYS OF EATING A DELICIOUS HONEY BUN?"

The sexy muscular man helped her out of the wagon, as the dancers performed behind her. They danced in unison as she continued her song.

"THOSE WERE THE DAYS THAT WERE JUST PLAIN OLD FUN.

"SOUR APPLE STICKS AND LAY'S POTATO CHIPS."

The dancers threw bags of potato chips and tee shirts saying 'Creative Juices,' the title of Bianca's album into the crowd. The $5,000,000 endorsement deal with a camera company enabled Bianca to snap pictures with selected fans, as she sent them back into an audience who were dazzled and in awe.

> *"TWO LITER PEPSI, MCDONALD'S ORANGE OR ROOTBEER SODA,*
>
> *"GRAPE KOOL-AID WAS THE BEST AND THEN WE GOT OLDER."*

The crowd went nuts! Standing on their feet and dancing without a care in the world.

> *"THE CRAZY DANCES WERE FUN AND GREAT. Y'ALL REMEMBER THE SNAKE?"*

Bianca seemed to have so much fun doing that dance! Everyone in the place was on their feet, doing the snake and following her lead, as she doubled the motion to one side!

> *"JORDACHE JEANS FIT US TIGHT, GUESS WAS FLY.*
>
> *"CARAMEL BROWN TIMS FOR THE MEN.*
>
> *"BLOCK PARTIES ALL NIGHT WITHOUT A SINGLE FIGHT.*
>
> *"THREE'S COMPANY, BRADY BUNCH, REMEMBER MARSHA'S NOSE?*
>
> *"AND WHAT'S HAPPENING, GOOD TIMES, RICK JAMES - SUPERFREAK, LL AND HIS LOVEMAKING RHYME.*
>
> *"THOSE WERE THE DAYS THAT WERE JUST PLAIN OLD FUN."*

A few years back Bianca had felt like she had been running in a fifty-yard dash, at top speed, when someone had jumped out at the twenty-five-yard mark, and punched her in the face! Things had not gotten much better in her personal relationship since.

She put the papers aside as she sat in her new-age, nine-projector home office, recalled her life, and wondered how it had railwayed into such a negative personal life, while at the same time, such a positive professional life. Although her parents raised their children to believe anything was doable, Bianca now started to doubt them.

Bianca is the eldest of five siblings: Delaney Baxter-Livingston, a journalist; Dr. Armani Baxter; soon to be Attorney Adar Baxter; and amateur singer Britney Baxter, who lived a rather lavish lifestyle in Southern California. Bianca looked around her office at her Grammy's, MTV, and Video Music Awards on her wall, before looking down at her photo in the newspaper. She was 5'4 and weighed 107 pounds. Her skin, with its reddish clay undertone, was magnified by the sun, in a way that accentuated her butterscotch complexion. Almond-shaped eyes, perfect white teeth, long silky jet-black hair (from her mom's side of the family), had always given her the strength to project the self-confidence her parents raised all of their children to have. Slowly and from deep within, this confidence had begun to dwindle.

It was at the City Club that Bianca was discovered by Millennium Records' Vice President of A&R, Ricky Simmons. Shortly after her contract was signed six years ago, they started dating.

With a $90,000 advance from Millennium, Bianca gave her family and best friend Mia a small token of appreciation. She felt it only right to give Mia money because she had stayed with Mia and her family for a few years, rent-free. Bianca took out a loan, purchased a small condo in the Hancock Park section of the mid-Wilshire district, and then invested the rest. At the time, $90,000 seemed like $1,000,000 to Bianca. When her albums went platinum and her acting career began to blossom, the money started flowing heavily. Her brother Adar's alcoholic fraternity brother did some contractual research and had her contract revamped.

Her money worries were over. She moved into a 12-bedroom mansion in the Pacific Palisades near Malibu, with an indoor and outdoor pool, a few huge Jacuzzis, and a tennis court. Later she installed an indoor bowling alley with neon lights. Once she saw the 1,200 square foot master bathroom she knew she had to have the house. One of the walls in her bedroom was an actual waterfall, like she had seen in upscale restaurants in Japan. It was truly amazing. She and Ricky couldn't believe it. She felt so peaceful when she entered the luxurious estate! At first making the house feng shui friendly was Bianca's primary focus in decorating her new home. However, it soon became annoying trying to keep up with the rules of positioning. Most of the furniture was purchased in Italy while she was on tour. Bianca had always told herself she would shop in Italy when she got rich and famous. For years she had asked her parents for subscriptions to furniture magazines as Christmas gifts. By the time she was eighteen, she knew about Frau, Intervista, Matt Nikel Plated Steel, Opal Glass, etc. She knew about the coating of clear plastic, the difference between cheap wood and high-end wood. The years and years of devouring magazine after magazine had enabled her to mentally develop a style of her own. Those images repeatedly resurfaced as she lovingly decorated her home. Bianca and her sisters traveled to Atlanta to shop for furniture at Haufmans, a quaint little store that catered to a celebrity clientele. Her mom always said everyone should love going home. Bianca slowed down when she hired her maid/cook, Rocki.
"Miss Baxter, you are going to need a bigger house," she would say.
Bianca decided she needed to reign in her desire to spend. She started to become more selective in her purchases, however if some delectable piece of furniture, planted itself into the far corners of her mind, she became powerless to resist. This elusive thought helped to curve her spontaneous habits.

Bianca hired Rocki to come in six days a week. Born in Jamaica and raised by a Filipino mom, Bianca met Rocki in her doctor's office. Rocki, a divorced forty-five-year-old, short, stubby woman with beautiful Brazilian brown colored skin was there with Mrs. Rivers, a highly acclaimed actress similar to Audrey Hepburn. When Mrs. Rivers was called in to see the Doctor, she and Rocki engaged in a conversation about life and careers. Rocki vaguely knew who Bianca was. She had been a nanny and maid for Mrs. Rivers and her wealthy husband. When the Rivers decided to move to New York to be closer to their two grown daughters, Rocki had three weeks to decide what she was going to do. The Rivers offered her continued employment in New York, but Rocki wanted to stay on the West Coast to be close to her own daughter. When Rocki mentioned she had also cooked for the Rivers Bianca knew she had to ask her to work for her. Shocked, but happy, Rocki agreed to work for Bianca. The following week, Bianca met with Mr. and Mrs. Rivers. They spoke highly of Rocki and expressed relief that their move would not inconvenience her unnecessarily. Though Bianca's gut had made her trust Rocki even in the doctor's office, it was comforting to have her credentials validated. Her mom, Supreme Baxter, had often told her children, not everyone you meet is crazy.

Recognizing her own innocence, Bianca decided to fly her mom and sister Delaney out to Los Angeles to give her their stamp of approval. They, too, loved her. Rocki worked out great. She had one daughter who was twenty-four and was a big fan of Bianca's. The daughter, who had completed two years at Santa Rosa Junior College, worked as an assistant for a veterinarian hospital, and lived with her father. Rocki was happy her daughter had finally done something productive with her life. She didn't mind that she hadn't completed a four-year college. Her daughter had gotten hooked on black beauties and crank several years back and traveled down a long road to recovery.

Bianca use to say she didn't want someone to come in everyday because she had wanted to maintain the self-sufficiency her parents had instilled in her as a child. It was her little hang-up. She didn't want to turn into the Hollywood pretentious pre-madonna whose purpose was to keep up with the Katz's! *Hollywood was full of the, 'have to have a nanny, drive a luxury car even if I can't afford it, may have to lease it or live in it!'* attitudes. She simply didn't want to become that ugly person. However, with the traveling, studio sessions, movie sets and shows, she became too tired, and worn out to clean her own house or cook. She decided she would be totally self sufficient for at least one day out of the week.

One thing that didn't pose a conflict for her was her continued desire to invest her money wisely. Bianca was grateful for her dad's investment skills. "Don't trust those California light bulb folks! They will rob you blind," he always said. "They are always smiling for no apparent reason. Don't trust them. They are smiling because they are prepping you before they bop you with a scam!" Bianca would just laugh. He had felt this way about Californians since she was little, so she accepted it. She realized people didn't change unless it was beneficial to them.

Years earlier, according to Bianca's father, one of his bosses, who happened to be from California, had made a practice of smiling and acting real concerned about company morale. He frequently used this excuse to write up many of his subordinates, usually for something petty or miscellaneous. He developed a cancerous legion and moved back to California. Joseph Baxter was ecstatic, not because his former boss had developed a terminal illness, but because this man was out of his life. Ever since then he never trusted people from California. Actually his paranoia had kept Bianca's bank account and investments on point financially.

According to her accountant, 30-year-old Bianca is worth $70,000,000 and still climbing. However, she wished her personal life were equally as golden. She had been in this shady relationship and hadn't seemed to shake Ricky, she thought while she studied one of her best photos in a magazine.

Her best friend Mia said she was a late bloomer. She called it the *P to the 4th Power Syndrome*. This simply meant that while her *P*rofessional life continued to *P*rosper, her *P*ersonal life was *P*athetic.

This was it for her. It was really bothering Bianca that Ricky was so ungrateful and unappreciative of who she was, and what she was about. She felt like she had stuck by this man through thick and thin. Lately, times were more thin than thick! She was glad she sent him that horrible email. The words sorry, son of a bitch rang in her head, loud and clear!

Then the sweeter side of her personality kicked in for a second, as she remembered, she had gone to church on Sunday. She had promised God she would pray for the ones who tried to harm her character and reputation. She had found it extremely difficult to keep this vow, and had experienced a few relapses of cruel thoughts. She asked God for forgiveness, then mumbled Ricky deserved it!

CHAPTER 2
DRAMA
RICKY

"What the hell is her problem? I can't believe she would have the audacity to put this shit on my email."

"Who are you talking about?" asked Scooter who was sitting in Ricky's office. They were listening to some new music from one of Ricky's artist.

"Bianca, she sent me an email. She doesn't know who can see this."

"Well, is it bad?" asked Scooter, looking curious.

"Hell yeah, she has truly lost her damn mind. I don't know what she was thinking. I'm not getting back with her this time. She is crazy. Man, read this shit."

Scooter got up and went over to Ricky's computer. He read the email. "Wow man, this is deep. Didn't she see Enemy of the State?" he laughed.

Ricky didn't find his statement funny. Out of all of the times that they had broken up, she had never gone this far as to put their business in the streets. She knew people at his office were nosy as hell, especially Ricky's assistant. They use to joke about company owners reading their employees emails. He decided he was not calling her.

"Ricky, what did you do to her this time?" Scooter stood up looking at him like he was crazy.

"I didn't do shit to her. You know, brothers try to cater to sisters' needs, be there for them, buy them expensive shit, take care of them in the bedroom and this is what we get in return, DRAMA. I don't know why she put her thoughts on email. We've been together for almost six years and all of a sudden she can't talk to me? We both work in the music business and I have to be out late at night and sometimes it happens to be with women. I don't know why her silly ass is tripping. What the hell."

"You didn't tell me you all had broken up," Scooter said while walking back to his seat across from Ricky's desk.

"That's because she breaks up with me every other week."

"That's true," said Scooter.

"I'm getting tired of this shit." He stared at his navy blue apple laptop in the large office located at the end of the hall, fuming. He read the email over and over again in a matter of minutes.

"When did she send it?" asked Scooter breaking the silence.

"I saw it go through on my blackberry about a week ago but I ignored it. Being on the road is killing me. I still can't believe she did this. I should call her up and curse her the fuck out."

At thirty-two years old, Ricky, according to Ebony Magazine, is a top record company executive. Working for Millennium Records for almost nine years, the company had many platinum artists under their belt, thanks to him. "Why do I have to go through the bull? I know I still look good! I don't have time for this mess. I have major issues if you allow Bianca to describe me."

"You are crazy, man." Scooter laughed. "You really think that you're God's gift to women!"

"Seriously, I'm a pretty boy! You know, I resemble Jayson Williams, who used to play for the New Jersey Nets, although my body is not as thick or toned as his." He looked at his reflection in the large fish tank by the window that overlooked Los Angeles and Beverly Hills. "I don't think Bianca really understands how much other women are sweating me and I chose her. She and Mia use to say, had I taken another path in life and gone to college, I would have been Kappa Alpha Psi material. Not that I need her and her best friend to validate who I am," Ricky quickly added.

"I see your vocabulary has increased since you've been with Bianca!" Scooter chuckled.

"Why do you keep making jokes when you know I'm pissed off?" Ricky snapped.

"Chill, Cuz. Relax. You are too uptight," said Scooter.

Scooter, Ricky's cousin, at thirty-four, was 5'8" and weighed 165 pounds. His physical appearance, although good, was not up to par with Ricky's.

"As I was saying," Ricky continued with his soliloquy. "I'm a top producer in L.A. and have produced platinum and triple platinum tracks on over a dozen albums."

"Did I mention the ladies love my widow's peak?" Scooter interjected and got up to look in the mirror.

"A woman would feel like becoming a widow if she hooked up with you!" Ricky cut in. "With your dead ass! Ha ha, laugh at that." Scooter laughed as if his confidence could not be budged as he turned around and went back to his seat. "You are one of those guys women say, 'He would be cute if he were taller!" Both men laughed harder.

"It is evident that you're trying to take the pressure off yourself. You're tripping hard. This is the hand I was dealt with so I have to live with it. As long as I have money in my pocket, I'm happy," said Scooter.

"Your point is what?" Asked Ricky.

"Ricky, my point is, it doesn't matter what you have accomplished in life if your spirit and soul are whack," Scooter said as he reached into his pocket to take out his Chapstick.

"I don't want to talk about my soul and my spirit right now. Do you have to get deep on me all of the time?" Ricky wondered why Scooter was telling him all this nonsense. "You have been doing this since we were kids. Damn corny ass!" he mumbled. "Let's discuss Bianca's psyche and what her damn problem is."

"Why can't you stop kidding yourself and call her?"

Ricky sighed. "I'm not going to lie. It is bothering me. It is actually killing me because I want to call her and curse her out, but I'm going to be the bigger person and let this ride out. I'm not calling her. Later for her." Ricky paused for a second. Then he continued. "See in Brooklyn, back in the day, I would have gone over to her house, knocked on the door and when she opened it, punched her in the face and just walked away without saying a word."

"I know, man, but you are not back in Brooklyn," said Scooter. "You have come a long way from that. Plus, you really love this girl. Just call her. I have to break out." He got up and reached across Ricky's desk to slap him five. "I will catch up with you later, Cuz."

"Later, man."

Ricky decided he would reminisce on the days in Brooklyn later on.

He stared at his email a little longer, burning inside. He allowed the anger to get the best of him. He then dialed her private line.

'No one is available to answer your call at the moment, so please leave...' Click. He hung up and called her agency's private line. The telephone rang several times.

CHAPTER 3
SISTER TO SISTER
BIANCA

Bianca had a big knot in her stomach. She hadn't eaten all day, which she knew was stupid because she needed to eat to take her medication. She had landed in Los Angles earlier in the morning and wanted to relax. It felt good for her to lie around for once, and do nothing. However, she needed to get back to rehearsing her lines. She picked up the phone to call Britney first. Britney always had a nasty disposition on life; therefore she could call her to hear something negative! She answered the phone on the first ring.

"Hello. I'm leaving now," said Britney

"Hey Britney, what are you doing?"

"Hey big sis, I thought you were Samantha or Tedra."
Bianca rolled her eyes at Tedra's name-she was named after her father Ted. Black folks can be a trip sometimes with the name's thing.

"Tedra. I thought you two had a fight?"

"We did, but we made up."

"But you slept with her man."

"They weren't together anymore and she doesn't know that for sure."

"Didn't one of your other friends tell her?"

"Yes, but we are not friends with her anymore."

"Whatever." Bianca decided to change the subject. "What are you doing?"

"I'm trying to find my other Bottega Veneta boot. The ones you gave me because they didn't look good on you. I really want to wear them."

"Your other boot? Where are you going?"

"I'm going to this industry dinner party in New York with Samantha and Tedra. The record company is going all out."

"Oh yeah, who is the artist?" Bianca asked.

"EXiT. The label is introducing their second album."

"Really, that is great. I just saw them at a function last week. Are you going to speak to them?"

"We probably will."

"Tell them I said hey!"

"Okay. What's up with you? How are you?"

"I'm okay, I guess."

"You guess?" Bianca imagined Britney running her fingers through her long fake weave. Britney was the color of a ripe mango.

"Hold on so that I can slip on the black cocktail dress you gave me the last time I visited L.A.!" There was some shuffling on the phone. "Good, I found my other stiletto boot." Her voice faded in and out. "Now sis, I can't talk that long because the girls are waiting for me."

"What else is new? Well, I won't keep you. You go ahead and have a good time."

"Okay, maybe I'll call you when I get in later on tonight. With the time difference, it won't be too late. Are you going to be home?"

"Probably."

"Okay, I'll speak to you later."

They hung up.

Bianca dialed Armani's number and got the answering machine. He was probably at the hospital. She then tried calling Adar. The phone rang twice and she hung up figuring he was out studying. She wondered where her cousin Shana was. Not that she would tell her big mouth cousin her business. As she sat and pondered, her conclusion hit her, maybe it was best not to tell her brothers either. She knew they would probably want to catch a flight to L.A. and handle Ricky in a not so positive way. Her best friend Mia was probably in the library studying her law books as usual. Mia felt like, since this was her second time around going back to law school, she would really dive in and take it seriously. Bianca decided to call Delaney. She usually listened without asking tons of questions. She'll be more sympathetic in a sisterly-womanly way. Mia would grill her until Bianca told her, and she wasn't ready to tell anyone everything. Being indecisive was becoming a natural thing for her lately.

Bianca dialed Delaney's number.   After the fourth ring she was just about to hang up when Bryce answered the phone. "Hellwo," he said with his cute little raspy voice.   Delaney said he was now missing his two front teeth.

"Hi Bryce, its Aunty Bianca. How are you?"

"I'm fine, Aunty Bianca."

"What are you doing?"

"I'm talking to Aunty Britney."

"Oh yeah. I just got off the phone with her."

"I asked Daddy if I could call her. She said she was getting ready to go out."

"Well, click over to the other line and tell her to call you when she gets back. I need to speak with your mommy. Is your mommy home?"

"Yes, Mommy's home. Hold on."

He clicked over to the other line.   Bianca started to reminisce about the last time she had seen her cute little nephew while waiting for him to come back to the other line.   She envisioned him with his cocoa brown complexion and big dark eyes and long girlie eyelashes.   The last time she saw him, he was three and a half.   Gosh, that was a year and a half ago. Things had changed. Bianca had visited Boston for shows, but not as often as she would have liked.

"Hellwo, Aunty Bianca...."

"I'm here. Have you been a good boy?"

"Yes, I have been a really good boy. You can even ask Mommy."

"I believe you. What are you doing?"

"I was getting ready to color before I called Aunty Britney."

"Where is your mommy?

"She is upstairs."

"Can I speak to her?"

"Hold on." He put the phone down. Bianca could hear him running up the stairs as he yelled, "M-o-m-m-y, the telephone, it's Aunty Bianca." She could hear Eric, her brother in-law yelling in the background for Bryce to stop running through the house.   The tone of his voice was stern and authoritative. It matched his build.

Eric was 6'2" and the color of beautifully shellacked wood. Their television was loud.   The weather portion of the news was on. *'Cloudy with a chance of heavy rain later on this evening,'* said the weatherman in the background.   Boston always did have sucky weather. They had literally one week of summer!

Eric picked up the phone.   "What's up sister in-law? How are you?"

"I'm okay. How are you?"

"I'm great.   I can't complain.   I have a beautiful wife and a healthy energetic son."

They laughed.   He yelled for Delaney to pick up the phone.

Eric and Delaney had been married for almost seven years and he still adored her. He was a great husband and an excellent father.   They had the storybook relationship. Eric and Delaney met in Boston in undergrad.   Delaney went to Northeastern University and pledged AKA Sorority, Incorporated and Eric went to Boston University and pledged Phi Beta Sigma Fraternity, Incorporated.   They dated throughout college and had a beautiful wedding shortly after graduation. They decided to stay in Boston because Eric got accepted to Harvard Law School.

Bianca's parents paid for the wedding and Eric's parents bought them a nice little colonial, three-bedroom house in Cambridge, near Harvard Square as a wedding gift. When Delaney announced she was pregnant, both families were ecstatic because Bryce was going to be the first grandchild. Delaney decided to take some time off with the baby and later got her masters in journalism and became a reporter for the Boston Globe.   Eric started his own law firm after school with two of his frat brothers. They called it Universal Esquire.

"Hello."   Twenty-nine-year-old Delaney picked up the phone from upstairs.   She too, had the almond-shaped eyes with a beautiful caramel complexion with West Indian high cheekbones.

"Hey Delaney."

"Hey lady."

Just before Eric got off of the phone he reminded Bianca that she promised to attend Bryce's birthday party this year. She agreed and said she would definitely be there even if she had to walk!

"What's wrong?"

"Nothing, I'm a little down."

"Why, what happened?" Delaney sounded concerned.

"I just broke up with Ricky."

"Again? Oh, I'm sorry." Her tone did a downward spiral.

"I'm really trying not to get back with him this time. It's hard, though."

"Well, why don't you come out here for a few days so we can take your mind off him? We'll go shopping, rent movies, talk and eat fattening foods!"

"I know, but I'm so swamped with trying to remember my lines for this upcoming film and attend engagements to promote my album."

"Maybe you should take some time off. Bianca, you have been working like a dog."

"I know and I'm tired, but the industry doesn't work like that. You have to work while you can. Nothing is promised."

"I know, but you sound so tired and burnt out. Are you really okay?"

"No, but I will be. Ricky feels like he can walk all over my heart and soul and I'm supposed to take it. Not this time. He has a womanizing problem. At times, he can be so sweet. Other times, I think he gets scared and feels like he has to sabotage things."

"I'm so sorry, Bianca," said Delaney. Bianca's private line clicked. She didn't answer it.

"I'm sorry, too. I don't want to talk about him anymore." Bianca immediately changed the subject. "How is the job? Is it getting any better?"

"No, the racism is getting worse. They are always trying to stick me with the stories in the urban community. Until I get a suburban gig, I have done my last story in Roxbury. I already spoke to Eric about it and he keeps telling me to quit."

"What is taking you so long?"

"Fear. We weren't raised to quit a job when things weren't going well. We were taught to stick it out."

"Not if the racism was blatant and unbearable. We were taught to stand up for ourselves. However, if Eric is telling you it is okay to do it, then what is the problem? Do you all have enough money saved?"

Bianca's private line clicked again. She still didn't pick up.

"The law firm is just now starting to see a profit. I don't want to struggle."

"Delaney, you have never had to struggle."

"Having to survive off of tuna fish is struggling."

"You've never had to do that."

"I know, but it sounded good!" They laughed.

"You will be fine. Quit. Seriously, I will give you money. You don't have to take that crap. You are a Baxter."

"I know, but you are always buying us expensive gifts and doing nice things for us. I enjoy getting up and going to work. I just don't like this particular job."

"Delaney, you have been passed over several times. Mom and Dad would be heated to know that you are settling in life."

"I know but I don't want Bryce to want for anything. Kids are expensive."

"I swear his feet grow every ten days! Not to mention the rest of his body. Bianca, you should see him, he keeps us laughing all of the time. Last week we parked the truck and took him on the train to go downtown. Bryce got a seat near the window while Eric and I stood in front of him. The train stopped and a heavyset woman got on. A few people got off at the stop. The woman came over to sit in the empty chair next to Bryce. As she sat down, the train suddenly moved and she let out a loud fart." Delaney laughed as she told the story as if she were having a flashback.

"Oh my goodness! What?" Bianca screamed, partly laughing.

"Yes, she accidentally farted and it was louddddd."

"I know Bryce had a field day with her." Bianca was cracking up.

"'Oooww, Mommy she farted!'" he said. "It took all of Eric's facial muscles not to laugh. I wanted to laugh, too, but I figured one of us had to be the adult." She started raising her voice in between laugher in order to complete the story. "I gave Bryce a dirty look and told him to be quiet."

'But Mommy, it stinks!' he said.

"I had to threaten to beat him. Eric stared at Bryce very hard and told him if he said one more word, he was going to get knocked out! Everyone on the train was staring at the lady and us. The woman was quite embarrassed. I didn't dare look at Eric because I would have cracked up."

Delaney was laughing so hard she was screaming and said that she had tears pouring down her face.

"What was the lady saying?" Bianca was trying to catch her breath from laughing so hard.

"Not a word. Her plump face was bright red. She frowned and stared straight ahead. We had to get off of the train at the next stop. We hurried off the train because Eric was starting to laugh and had to sit down. Bryce asked him why he was laughing so hard. He patted him on the head and told him that he was truly his son. I told him later on that night that I was glad I was there because he would not have been able to compose himself."

"What did he say?"

"He laughed."

"Darn, my line keeps ringing. Delaney, hold on, someone keeps calling both of my private lines."

"Okay." They were still chuckling like aftershocks from an earthquake.

"Hello."

"Hello, it's me," said Ricky. "I called you on your other line, but I guess you're not answering that line."

"Nope." Bianca's mood immediately changed. "The servants are out running errands. Why are you calling?" she snapped.

"I need to talk to you."

"Ricky, I don't want to talk and I'm on the other line."

"Okay, I'll hold on."

"I'm talking long distance."

"I said, I will hold on," he said in a stern voice.

"Hang on." She switched back to Delaney.

"Delaney, how long are you going to be home?"

"I'll be here for the rest of the day and evening."

"Okay, I'll call you back."

"Why, who is that?"

"It's one of the producers from my album." She lied.

"Okay, I'm here if you need me. I love you, big sis."

"Love you, too. Kiss Bryce for me. Don't forget, if you need money, I'm here. I'm serious about that. If you are as unhappy as you say you are, then you should think about quitting on Monday."

"Okay. I will seriously give it some thought."

"Keep Bryce away from farting folks!

"Hey, that is not nice," she said in a snickering voice. I'm glad you weren't with us!" They both chuckled.

"I will try and call you back later." Bianca hated lying. After speaking with Ricky, she knew she would be set back from thinking about the devastating state of mind her situation had put her in. There had been days when she was fine, but this was not one of them.

"Think about coming home for a restful visit."

"I will," she said, sort of preoccupied about what Ricky wanted.

"Chow."

"Bye." She clicked over to her other phone. "Yes?"

CHAPTER 4
FLASHBACK
RICKY

"Bianca, don't give me any bullshit about you being too busy because I know your damn schedule. I need to speak to you face to face."

"Ricky, I really don't have anything to say to you."

Ricky shut his office door and turned up his music in case he had to get loud, or even worse, indignant. He didn't want his subordinates or co-workers to hear. A hot new Hip-Hop song was playing in the background.

"Why would you send me that email? That was foul. Why would you put our business out in public like that? You know how this damn industry is."

Bianca attempted to respond but Ricky talked over her. "What if someone had intercepted the email? Then what?"

"It sounds pretty far fetched to me. Are you going to let me speak or are you going to continue to run your damn mouth like you always do?"

"What the hell is that suppose to mean?"

"Figure it out."

Click. Bianca hung up.

"No, she did not hang up on me!" Ricky mouthed out loud. He slammed the phone down, jumped up, turned off his computer and forcefully hit the stop button on the CD player. He then grabbed his cell phone and headed out the door and down the long corridor, passing by framed pictures and plaques of old and new Millennium artists. There was also a big picture of CEO, Tom Swindle on a wall by itself, not far from his secretary's desk.

His twenty-two year old secretary Roberta, was slightly smacking on her gum, while yapping on the phone, in her usual manner, as Ricky approached. Related to Jen, President of the company, she'd been hired while he was on vacation. Ricky felt this was an affront to him, because he and Jen had slept together, a long time ago. This was during his non-committal wild days prior to Bianca.

Roberta was a short, awkward-looking girl with a dusty brown complexion. The front of her hair was twisted to the middle and then met a horrible weave down the back. She was dressed like a ghetto girl who'd like you to believe she was classy. Her lipstick was doo-doo brown and her fingernails were long with a topaz color and a French white manicure on the tips. She could stand to tone down her voice a notch and could probably be described as a L.A. roach, which was worse than a New York chicken or pigeon head. She looked up over her desk and saw Ricky coming through the reflection of the glass. She told her personal caller to hold on.

Ricky stopped at her cubicle looking annoyed. "I'm leaving for a little while. If someone needs me and it's urgent, call me on my cell phone. I'll be back in a couple of hours. Oh yeah, make sure you're not so preoccupied with your personal calls that you can't answer my damn phone," Ricky said in an authoritative tone. Busted! He thought. Roberta's ghetto face cracked. Ricky disappeared into the elevator, pressed 'G' and before he knew it, was in the parking garage waiting for the valet to drive his truck around to the front. The valet came flying around the corner in his black Range Rover.

"Damn, slow down," he thought out loud. The valet stopped, got out and Ricky got inside while handing the valet a few bucks, then drove off. Ricky turned on the radio. It was programmed to KKBT, 100.3, The Beat. *Fortunate* was playing, surprisingly, on the hip-hop station. Ricky hated that song and abruptly turned the radio off. He needed to think in silence. He needed to think about what he was going to do about Bianca.

She was extremely articulate and it presented a problem only in arguments. Her words could really scare a brother. Screw it, Ricky thought. He was going to curse her the hell out and leave. Ricky hated to admit it right now, but he really cared about her stupid butt. Suddenly his cell phone rang. "Hello?"

"Ricky, I have Tiny for you."

"Take a message."

"I tried. She is insisting that she speak with you."

"I said to only call me if it's urgent. Should I rephrase my statement? The caller does not determine whether a call is urgent. You determine it. I don't care what she said. You know who should be classified as urgent. You didn't just start working for me."

"You have so many women calling, I don't know who is who. This woman said…"

Now Ricky was really pissed and cut her off. "I don't care what she said. Your job is to take messages for me, not to determine how many women call me. Do what the hell I ask you to do or someone else will. Now take a fucking message!" Ricky, really pissed now, ended the call, and continued to drive in silence, while sinking heavier into his thoughts. Fifteen minutes later, his phone rang again.

"Talk to me. This better be important," he said in an abrupt harsh voice as he pressed the button on the speakerphone.

"Hey Ricky, what's up? It's Armani. Are you busy?"

Ricky took a deep breath to get out of his zone.

"No, not really. I'm on my way over to your sister's house."

"Tell her I said, what's up."

"If she lets me in," Ricky mumbled.

"What?" Armani asked.

"Nothing." There was silence. Then they began to speak at the same time.

"How is….?"

"Where…?" Armani asked. "I'm sorry, man. What were you going to say?"

"I was going to say, how is the Capitol treating you? I know a couple of months ago, you weren't happy with it."

"I'm okay with it now. I guess I can't complain this week. I'm almost done with my residency. I guess it served its purpose!"

"How is that beautiful woman of yours?" Angie's face and body popped into his head.

"Angie is fine. I hardly get to see her because I'm at the hospital ninety percent of the time. She used to be understanding. Things seem to be changing."

"Changing, how?"

"Being so busy has put a strain on our relationship but I suppose we'll work through it. I'm use to the friction now and the no sleep part, but I'm not use to this newfound attention I'm getting from other women. I'm feeling a little funny about the living together thing."

"Well, when did you start feeling this way? It has been a few years."

"I've never cheated on her but it seems like girls are coming at me real strong now."

"It's because you're going to be on a doctor's salary. Girls are seeing dollar signs."

"Is that really true?" Asked Armani with the innocence of a virgin.

"Hell yeah, but Angie is fine as hell," said Ricky smiling from ear to ear.

"You are crazy."

"I know."

"She has a pretty chocolate face, a nice fly short haircut, beautiful bod…"

"Hey, hey, hey," Armani interjected. "I don't want to have to box you down for checking out my girl."

The two laughed. "Man, what I'm saying is that she is everything a man could ask for in a woman," Ricky said.

"My boys keep telling me to go for mines, but don't get caught. Adar keeps saying I would be a fool to mess this up. Especially judging from my track record."

Armani laughed. "I think if you are going to dibble, you'd better be good at it. You aren't."

"Don't start!"

"Seriously, you can't be careless. You have to cover your tracks because women have upgraded their cheating radar detectors!"

They both laughed loudly.

"Man, I didn't call to talk about me. What's up with you? How is the fake *you know what* music industry?" Asked Armani.

"It's going good, hectic as usual," said Ricky.

"Are you still not working and getting paid tons of money?"

"Brother, I work. They work me like a dog."

"Just because you went to school for forty years to work in a stinking hospital, it doesn't mean diddly to me," Ricky said as he let out a macho laugh.

"Somebody had to do it."

"I know, why not you! You're crazy man. I'm going to be in DC for a few days and then heading to New York. I had been meaning to call you but things have been chaotic on the West Coast, to say the least." Suddenly, Ricky wished that Armani wasn't Bianca's brother because he wanted to elaborate on the stressful problems they were having. However, he knew ultimately Armani would side with his big sister. Bianca hadn't told her family everything and Ricky didn't want to change the positive flow of their conversation. At the end of the day if the Baxter family knew how much drama Ricky had caused their precious sister, he would have to fight the upper-middle class Baxter brothers and the Dad as well.

"What's your schedule like?"

"When you do your residency that is your schedule. It is all work, work, work."

"I know that feeling. They got me traveling so much I should own stock in the airline industry!

Armani's phone beeped. "Hold on Ricky." Armani clicked over to the other line and immediately came back to Ricky. "Ricky, I have to go. Angie is calling from her cell phone."

"That's cool. Handle your business. I'll call you when I get there."

Ricky pressed 'end' then realized he couldn't speed up because traffic was thick on the 405. He knew he should have taken Sunset all the way down and thought about how much he hated L.A. for this very reason. A person sits in traffic for what seems like hours and never finds out what the hell caused the traffic in the first place! Suddenly Ricky was forced to slam on his brakes. "Damn it!" he said out loud as he blew his horn at a Mexican lady driving an old beige Nova, who had just cut him off. *Damn, I didn't know they still made those cars!* It reminded Ricky of Warren, one of his boys back in Brooklyn, and his old piece of shit Nova. Sometimes they could put it into reverse. Sometimes they couldn't! But they had good times in the hood driving around in that car, that is when it was acting right. He sure missed Brooklyn.

Do or Die BedStuy was what Ricky and his friends called Bedford Stuyvesant. Hancock, Ricky's block was cool, though. However, when one got to both corners, anything could happen. Between the drug dealers, crackheads, hoochies and strippers, Ricky didn't know which trafficking in the neighborhood was worse, but it was fun growing up in Brooklyn, especially in the summertime, until one of Ricky's boys was murdered.

Ricky, Warren and David were close like the young boys in Cooley High, that urban classic movie about four high school guys who were having fun being class clowns, chasing girls and enjoying the party life. They would sit on each other's stoops and check out people driving by in their phat cars. He and his friends would also watch the girls walking by with their Daisy Dukes on.

Ricky's cousin Scooter would come down from corny Queens, as they called it, and hang out with them sometimes, but he often said they were too wild, especially with all of the weed smoking and selling they did. Ricky always thought Scooter was square and too deeply into the music thing. Scooter received a drum set when he was eight years old. Then boredom set in when he was nine. His parents then purchased him a guitar one Christmas and later a violin for his birthday. His dad realized early on Scooter's love for music as well as his natural talents. His parents set up an eight-track studio in their basement and that's when Scooter's raw talent sizzled. He would record a song from the radio and add his instruments to reinvent the song. Then he would host a talent night at his house starring him!

Ricky, Warren and David messed around with a lot of chicks and had a system down pack. If a girl was EF (extra fly) and seemed somewhat intelligent and clean, they were in there, naked and free! That's when sex was just ridiculously accessible. They had no feelings for any of them. They were the flyest brothers on the block, even with Warren's busted car! They wouldn't even take the chicks to a real restaurant. The boys would go to one of the Bodegas on the corner right before they hopped on the train from walking around the village. That was when the hooptie was acting up. It was foul they knew, but whatever. Spending money on chicks was not acceptable in their pack. Accepting their money was almost like a ritual.

Ricky went back in heavy thought feeling like he had come a long way from his Brooklyn days. His attention drifted back to the freeway full of eccentrics on the roads going to auditions, the beach, lunch or simply nowhere.

The night Warren was shot and killed by some sucker named Blinky, over a girl, was really wild. Warren was seeing this chick named LaQueena, who they later found out, had a man in prison. He found out LaQueena was screwing Warren and had her set him up. She was giving the choice of dying herself or setting up Warren. She invited him over for what he thought was some *you know what,* then told him she would be right back. She said that she wanted to run to the corner store to play the numbers before it was too late. There was a knock at her door. Warren thought she didn't bring her key and opened the door. He was shot seven times. LaQueena's crumb snatchers were in their beds. They slept through the whole ordeal. Some kind of mother, Ricky thought. They always knew she was scandalous, but not low enough to set a brother up to be murdered.

Warren and Ricky were supposed to hang out later that night, but Ricky never heard from him. He first thought Warren had turned a quickie into an all night thang! He had given him silent kudos! The next day Ricky beeped him. No returned call. Then people in the neighborhood started talking about what happened. That is how it was in the ghetto. Gossip on the street was their form of CNN!

Ricky walked swiftly, with an uneasiness feeling in his stomach, down to Warren's house and knock on the door. His sister opened the door with an ocean of tears pouring down her face. She and her mom and other sisters had just left the hospital and were on their way to the police station. She just had to get away, so she had left them, and came home. This was like a nightmare.

Ricky fell to his knees and cried like a baby. "Oh God, no, not my boy." His mind was racing. David must have heard around the same time and came running down to Warren's house, climbed the painted light peach colored stone steps two at a time. He stopped, looking stunned. He had to help Ricky get up off the stoop. Warren's sister was standing in the doorway crying profusely and looking completely hollow. David, always the strongest out of the three, was trying unsuccessfully to hold his tears back and be strong for himself and Ricky.

CHAPTER 5
HARD TIMES
RICKY

The next day Ricky took his gun out of the shoebox under his twin bed, hid it in his Polo jeans, and walked the ten long blocks to LaQueena's house. It was apparent she had moved. A torn black leather barstool was visible through the window of her first floor apartment, which was located on the same side as the Bodega. There were no curtains in the window, and the front door was slightly open. LaQueena knew she had better take her bae bae kids and get the hell out of there. Ricky vowed that if he ever saw that witch again, he would kill her on sight.

He jumped on the J train and rode it back and forth for hours thinking about the good times they shared and how he would miss his boy. "Death is final," he remembered mumbling. He stared through his dark shades, straight out the window, not knowing whether to cry or take his fist and punch it through the window. It hurt like hell.

From that day on Ricky swore he would never trust a female nor treat them with respect. Although he hadn't shown them much respect anyway, he vowed that now it would be worse. Ultimately, he got the short end of the stick for his ignorance, negative thoughts and actions. Due to his careless behavior, he never anticipated, he would end up struggling with a disease.

He tried to go to Warren's funeral but only made it to the steps of the church. David was already inside. They said he had passed out. People tried to get Ricky to go inside but he couldn't do it. His heart and legs wouldn't allow it. His mind was clouded. This was some fucked-up shit. He wanted to smoke the most potent weed ever known to man and drink himself into oblivion. One thing was for sure, for the first time in his life, he didn't want to be around any chicks.

From the steps of the church, he could hear his cousin Scooter leading the congregation in the song, Precious Lord.

Precious Lord, take my hand,
Lead me on, let me stand,

I am tired, I am weak, and I am worn;

Through the storm, through the night,
Lead me on to the light,

Take my hand, precious Lord,
Lead me home.

Ricky remembered hearing this song while standing on the corner with his boys selling weed. The church was down the street. On Fridays, the choir rehearsed the song often. David was the only one out of their little crew that had graduated to selling cocaine and was also the only one to have been arrested for drug and gun possessions. Ricky didn't realize he knew the words. He wondered why this was happening in his life and how he could ever recover. He had never felt pain like that before. He wanted God to take the pain away. Shoot, he wanted God to take *him* away.

About a year after Warren's death, David was coming from the courthouse in Manhattan around mid-afternoon. He stopped in a nearby Bodega to buy a Newport Lucy, the single cigarettes sold. His nerves were shot to hell. He wanted to smoke a joint but didn't have anything on him. As he was pulling out his money, he heard a familiar voice. The fiery rage started in his toes and began to crawl up through his legs to the back of his neck.

"You are not getting all of that junk food. Put it back," said the familiar voice.

"Sir, that will be one dollar," said the Chinese man, for what he found out later was the third time he'd recited his statement. The steam and red horns had consumed his mind for what seemed like an eternity.

David turned around to see where that cringing voice was coming from. It was like a movie put in slow motion. That bitch LaQueena.

"You killed my boy," he remembered saying. It was as if he were on the outside watching himself beat this girl nearly to death in front of her oldest child; who looked to be in shock, after trying to help her mother and getting in the crossfire of a steel fist. He could see the few customers running out of the store with frightening looks on their faces. It was as if he were having an out-of-body experience. He could see the terror in LaQueena's eyes and the thick red blood gushing down her face.

"You will suffer like Warren suffered, bitch," he remembered saying.

She opened her mouth to scream, but her voice kept fading in and out.

David said he had clearly snapped. Blood was coming out of her mouth and she was then unconscious. The storeowner had apparently called the police. He said when the police got there, he must have still been beating her because he could hear voices saying things like, "Hold him down, you got his arm? Grab his leg. Use the stun gun on him, man. Use the pepper spray. We got a wild one." People had crowded around outside to see what was going on.

He said that first squirt of pepper spray brought him back to reality. He fell backwards and his first reaction was, *damn, what the hell happened here? What did I do?* He thought to himself as he grabbed his eyes while falling to the floor in excruciating pain.

LaQueena laid there in a pool of blood, not moving. Her daughter was screaming, "Mommy, please wake up. Somebody wake my mommy up." A dirty blonde haired short barbie-look-alike policewoman held her tight as if she were her own.

As they cuffed him and stuffed his head into the police car, David yelled out, "I hope you are dead, bitch. That will teach your crusty behind not to set people up. May your daughter mourn like Warren's mother, father and sisters mourned." News cameras were everywhere.

The police were interviewed and said that he looked to be in a drug daze. His bail was set at $100,000. Shortly afterwards he was on his way to prison for attempted murder. He wanted to come face to face with LaQueena's boyfriend but as it turned out he was in solitary confinement, for killing a Puerto Rican inmate over a cigarette. LaQueena was in a coma for several months. They learned this from the news. As they learned more details through the media, Ricky silently acknowledged they were good for something even if they did exaggerate the truth.

When David first got arrested, his dad, Warren's dad and Ricky went to visit him at the Brooklyn House of Detention for Men on Atlantic Avenue. David's mom was too hurt to go. She went the first few times he had gotten arrested but this time it was too much to bare. The men had to wait for hours at first, because David wouldn't come downstairs. His dad got into an argument with the Corrections Officers because it was taking so long. The officers tried to explain to him they had notified David, but he hadn't made it downstairs yet. Eventually the father was made to leave, for he loudly refused to believe David knew he was there, and wouldn't come out of his cell. Ricky stayed as long as he could, but visiting hours were soon over, so he left in a state of confusion, and fear for David's safety. David's father and Ricky made several attempts to visit him, with no luck. Ricky was baffled. David's father was pissed. David's mom contacted his Public Defender. He too, told the family that David was aware of their visits, but for some reason, chose not to come downstairs.

Almost a month later Ricky got a collect call from David. Luckily he answered the phone because his mom would have never accepted the charges. David had spoken to his family right before calling Ricky. He had been moved to Rikers Island and later moved again. He didn't sound too well.

CHAPTER 6
RIKERS ISLAND
RICKY

Ricky had to take a few trains and a bus to actually get onto the island. He wanted to punch the hell out of David when he saw him, but David had looked so frazzled and disheveled. Plus he was still his boy from way back. They had been through a lot.

When Ricky got onto the island he had to go through the long visitor line and show his ID. He stopped at packaging and left him $25.00. Ricky knew, being a welfare weed dealer, it wasn't much. He hadn't been selling as much. With the devastating turn of events he opted to stay in the house and think. There were several notices, flyers, and rules and regulations on the wall at the prison. There were two Amnesty boxes at different checkpoints. There was an actual option to dispose of your drugs or any other illegal items. Ricky went through the magnetometer to the visiting area. The chairs were light blue, hard and very uncomfortable on the buttocks. Ricky had gotten fidgety and nervous because after an hour, he wasn't sure if David was really going to come downstairs. He went to the snack machine twice, once to get some chips, the second time to get a Pepsi. He sat back down and observed the room. There was a large recycle bin in one corner, and lockers on the left wall for visitors to store extra clothing, belts, shoelaces, etc. There was a sign that read: NO AIR NIKE SNEAKERS. NO VELCRO SHOES. There were framed pictures on the wall that a visitor told him were made by inmates. Girls were entering with mini skirts just below their butts and high heel shoes. He saw lots of chicks he wanted to take into the bathroom and tear them up. He knew it was inappropriate but took a few phone numbers anyway. The situation seemed to agree with his convenient philosophy, there is nothing like new booty! After determining David wasn't going to show up, he decided to leave and wouldn't come back for a few weeks.

"RICKY SIMMONS, THE INMATE IS HERE. PLEASE REPORT TO THE BLACK GATES."

There was a bit of fear of the unknown in his heart. He turned to go to the black gate in the opposite direction. "Shit, it's about time," he mumbled.

He walked past one gate and heard the horrible sound of metal doors locking behind him. He was then standing in an area that was 200 square feet. There was another black gate in front of him. This gate opened and as he stepped out, he had to immediately put his left hand under a light to show the stamp that had been put there earlier. There was a tinted booth on the left with Correctional Officers inside. As he entered the 600-square-foot room, he saw around 45 multicolored little kid chairs and tables. He sat down and David came through the other side of the black gates. Ricky immediately stood up.

"Hey man, how are you?"

"I'm here. Trying to maintain."

They hugged. David had on a gray jumpsuit. His eyes looked dark. His skin looked ashy, not because he didn't bathe, but because of the stress. He looked tired and worn out to the max.

"How are you really?"

"I have been trying not to think about my situation. I'm sorry you and the fam came to visit and I didn't come down. I just needed some time to think. They gave me this bullshit, court-appointed Attorney and I have been so frustrated. He keeps telling me to plead guilty to get a lesser sentence."

"Don't do that. He's just trying to get out of doing the legwork."

"It doesn't matter, I'm fucked."

Just as David said that, a Corrections Officer yelled for the people next to them to put some distance between them. One girl, clad in a short skirt, had sat on one of the tiny tables; legs spread wide open, she'd begun to gyrate her body back and forth, while her man's face moved closer in the direction of her crotch. Hearing the Officer's command, she backed off the table, and the poor guy's face looked like a starving puppy whose food had just been taken away. Ricky was thankful he was a free man. David and he looked at each other, then continued on with their conversation. In any other situation they would have laughed but they didn't because they both knew how David felt or would eventually feel.

David said he was doing well. Ricky told him he had left him $25.00 and would send him some more money when he could.

"Anyone tried to tap that anus?" Ricky said half jokingly but truly serious to break the ice.

"Hell no!"

He almost wanted to be in there with him, but David wasn't entirely without some allies. There were also brothers, from around the way, that from time to time, they had hung out, and smoked weed with. Ricky asked David what kind of time the Judge had given him. David kept saying everything was pending. He had a feeling David knew but didn't want to tell him. Ricky apologized for not being in court for him. He couldn't watch his friend go down. David understood. He knew Ricky loved him. Everything was happening way too fast. Ricky felt like he was going crazy all over again.

"Wow, the time went by quickly."

"I know."

"Man, thanks for visiting me. I really appreciate it."

"You're like a brother to me." David got up from the chair. Ricky felt as though his spirit and soul were gone.

The last thing David communicated to Ricky was in a low and steady voice.

"Ricky, I have no regrets about my actions. I should have killed that stinking bitch."

Ricky was speechless. At that moment, they were as close as twins because he felt his pain wholeheartedly.

LaQueena came out of the coma for a few days and then suddenly died. Ricky thought to himself, *damn, be careful what you ask for.* Shortly afterwards, David was transferred again. This time to begin serving a life sentence.

CHAPTER 7
LIFE
RICKY

Ricky's life had changed drastically within two years. He went from macking with his two best friends to relying solely on himself. Warren's father sat him down and had a long heart to heart talk about life and living in the ghetto. Ricky didn't mean to cry but he did. It happened and he embraced it.

"Let it all out, son. You haven't cried since my son's funeral, huh?"

"No," Ricky told him. The last few years had been a blur to me. Too much had happened for a person his age to deal with. Warren's dad told him to straighten up his life, finish school, get a job and take it one day at a time. He said they would never forget Warren. He encouraged him to move on with his life and not let it pass him by. He said he wished he would have had the talk with David and him before David messed up his life. Soon after their talk, Warren's dad left his mother and sisters to never return.

Word on the streets was he was admitted into a mental institution. Some said he got hooked on drugs. Others said he became a wanderer. He couldn't handle it. He obviously took it harder than anyone ever knew. Eight months later he was found dead in an abandoned building with a crack pipe in one hand and Warren's baby picture in the other. In the ghetto, shit happened and everyone learned not to question it.

After months of trying to digest Warren's father's words, death, and Ricky's diagnosis, he started hanging out with his corny cousin Scooter more. His mom mortgaged her house to get Ricky the proper medications and care he needed. Ricky was scared and stressed. He was surprised his mom paid for anything dealing with him because it often appeared as if she didn't care about his life. Scooter was doing a lot of what seemed to be the corny music stuff but it was something to take Ricky's mind off of his life or lack thereof.

He hadn't known the scope of Scooter's talents until he heard him sing at the funeral and later watched him work in the studio. He was amazed at how talented he was, and with his leadership and business skills. Scooter invited Ricky to go to the studio one night. He said he had been dealing with some heavy music hitters.

"Yeah, right." Ricky told him. "What the hell do you know about heavy hitters?"

"Whatever, man. I know a helluva lot more than you do. If you want to come, cool. If not, that's cool too."

"Okay, what the hell. I'm not doing anything but sitting in my room getting lit."

Ricky's life consisted of smoking weed during the day and selling it at night. It was a conflict of interest, but shit, he wasn't perfect. Plus his Mom was getting on his nerves about looking for a job. He barely graduated from Brooklyn Tech. Early on he didn't think he was going to get accepted. There were so many brilliant Asian people, he wasn't sure if there was room for him. He felt his mom should have given him a break. At 16 he had endured a lot. He had wanted to go to Boys and Girls High School but his mom was completely against it. She said he had to take the test to get into Brooklyn Tech and he had better pass it. Because she acted so apathetic at times, he really hadn't thought she would care if he passed or not. He never had educational confidence in himself. In his mind you had to be smart to get into the Tech. When he passed the test he was first shocked then elated. When he told his mom, she acted exactly as he thought she would, uninterested.

"Good. I knew you would." She raised an eyebrow while reading the National Enquirer, drinking her coffee and smoking her Newport Lights cigarettes.

As he got older, Ricky realized his mom was bugging about her silly violent husband not being around, then when he was around, Ricky guessed he wasn't hitting it right or not at all!

"Are you going to turn out messed up like your father?" His mom, Janet Simmons-Johnson would ask. Janet was a banana color, 5'5 with dyed light brown hair. She use to be fly.

"What is that suppose to mean? Never mind, don't answer the question," he would snap back. His Step-Dad was crazy. He was constantly fighting with him for putting his hands on his mother. His mother continued to encourage him to hang out with Scooter after Warren's death. She felt that he was optimistic and doing positive things. Little did she know he had already started hanging out with him. It was not worth telling her. He didn't want to hear the old, *I told you so.* One day she made him so sick he gathered his things, phoned Scooter, and told him he would meet him at the studio. At that time, he didn't realize that this would be the beginning of what would be a success story, but only in his professional life.

Scooter was serious about his music. "No, I think the music should come in at this point. It sounds good but I think we should do one more take."

Ricky had found his passion in life. He could feel the music in his soul as well as his future. He started going with Scooter on a regular basis. He had seen a lot of celebrities go through the studio. He loved it so much he harassed Scooter to go in the studio everyday.

"Damn man, chill. You don't need to be paging me every day. I will let you know when the next session is."

Scooter introduced Ricky to several books like *HITMEN* and the *Music Business Handbook & Career Guide* to enlighten him about the music business. He eventually taught him how to use the boards, and how to read music and listen for certain instruments. He gave him insight on what the consumer looked for in music. Often times they were in the studio until six in the morning. Later, Ricky started imputing in various projects.

"Yo Cuz, you have a good ear," Scooter would say.

One night a top producer came into the studio. Scooter and Ricky were now a team, even though Scooter was the most knowledgeable by far. However, according to Ricky, to the chicks, they were a team! The producer lived in the Hollywood Hills and wanted them to do some work for him in California. *Wow*, Ricky thought, he couldn't wait to get to Hollywood, home of the stars and honeys roller-skating in bikinis.

"Yes."

"Chill Cuz," Scooter told Ricky.   "Sir, we have to discuss it amongst ourselves. Give us a number and we'll let you know in a few days." Scooter looked at Ricky with an evil eye to let him know to shut up. He had never been anywhere outside of Brooklyn, with an exception of Manhattan and its surrounding areas!   This was simply the lifestyle of a typical New Yorker.   Scooter eventually schooled him on how to conduct business.

"Don't be so desperate. People will rip you off faster than you can say your ABC's in this business if you act like you don't have anything going on. Even if you don't have anything going on, always act like you have something going on. I mean, don't get ridiculous. Act like a professional who is on point and unimpressed because you've seen it all."

Scooter did his investigative homework and they were on their way to Cali. The producer put them up in a real nice hotel. Hollywood was nothing like they had expected, but it was fun. They went back to pick up their belongings, and now only go back to visit family, or for business. Scooter had been back to visit his immediate family a lot, Ricky had only been back to visit his mom a few times. She had never been to California to visit him, and always made up excuses. Ricky figured she didn't want to leave her sorry man unattended. He kept telling her she was going to have a heart attack and possibly die at an early age if she continued to stress.

CHAPTER 8
FRIENDSHIP
BIANCA

Bianca's guest buzzer rang. She didn't feel like having company. She looked at the wall-mounted screen and nodded for Rocki to hit the *let in ok* button. Rocki waited five minutes, peeked out of the living room bay window, then opened the door with a big smile. Mia, chipper as usual walked in.

"Hey girl, I took a chance at coming over here," said Mia. "I was sort of in the neighborhood."

They hugged and Mia walked into Bianca's living room.

"You know it's okay. I'm so happy to see you. Come into the kitchen. Maria was just about to make me a salad. Did you eat?"

"I had eggs and beans earlier."

"Yuk!" Bianca had a disgusting look on her face. "You're still eating that crap-ola?"

"Yeah and it's good. I went to see Ronnie earlier this morning."

"How is little brother man?"

"He is as good as he can be. He said they are going to put him in the work release program. He is excited about that."

"Good for him."

"I hate to see my brother doing time because he really isn't a bad person."

"I know. Sometimes life throws a wrench in our program and messes it all up."

"Isn't that the truth?"

"I don't want to talk about Ronnie anymore. I can't change what happened in the past. So how the hell are you, B?"

"I'm okay. A little tired."

"I can imagine. You're on the road a lot. I was driving on the freeway and your song came on the radio, so I decided to come see my best friend."

"I'm glad you did," Bianca admitted.

"How is the industry treating you?"

"I still can't believe the direction my career has gone."

"Girl, I'm still so proud of you."

"Come into the kitchen and have some good food."

The two sat in Bianca's marble kitchen.

"I can't even go to the store without being noticed."

"Isn't that what you wanted?"

"Yeah, but sometimes I want to go to dinner or a movie without being harassed. Remember, years ago we were sitting in your bedroom trying to predict our future success?"

"Yes, I remember like it was yesterday."

"I never imagined that it would be like this."

"Yesterday you were moving your stuff into our house because you had to get away from the *bad roommates syndrome*." They laughed. "I kept telling you that four girls couldn't live together."

"Those were my girls. I met them at freshman orientation."

"So what, you met me sophomore year. Your point is what? They were jealous of you."

"For what? I didn't have anything. Must I tell you this for the one-hundredth time? I'm going to start charging you a fee! People can be jealous of you because you are YOU. You don't have to have anything or look better than them. You exude strength and beauty from within. You are charismatic, optimistic, intelligent, sexy…"

"Keep going!"

"I haven't even touched on your physical attributes. B, you're a special person. This is why God has blessed you with so much."

Am I really blessed? Bianca thought to herself. "Those were my girls."

"Past tense, they were your girls, said Mia. You outgrew them. Do you realize how long we have known each other? You moved to California almost fifteen years ago to attend UCLA and launch a singing career and you did it."

Gosh, Bianca thought to herself. She really did do it. She double majored in Music Theory and Business Marketing and minored in French. She developed a little name for herself while singing in the UCLA Gospel Ensemble and in grungy nightclubs around the Los Angeles area. After graduation, she and four of her college girlfriends moved into a large four-bedroom apartment in Westwood near the school. It turned out to be a huge mistake. The friendship was tainted beyond repair.

The first major problem was they had designated days for chores. Bianca always picked up the slack for a few of the girls. One girl was too tired to do her chores one week so she decided she would pick up the slack the next week. Dishes were always piled up in the kitchen. There were loud lovemaking noises at wee hours. Her clothes were being borrowed and never returned. There had been constant phone calls to the police because one girl had a boyfriend who's fists seem to always connect with her face. It was tiresome arguing over petty, childish issues. She finally confronted them and the drama escalated. The days were so stressful she gave them a 30-day notice and ended up moving out in one week.

Bianca moved to Compton with her best friend Mia and her family, whom she met sophomore year at an Oratory Competition. Being in Compton was certainly a cultural shock, having been raised in Jamaica Plain, Massachusetts, in a diverse upper middle-class neighborhood. Mia's house was small so Bianca had to sleep on the couch. Anything was better than her previous situation.

She loved living with Mia and her family. She finally had peace. Gina, Mia's mother became her California mom. Mia's grandmother Trucey, was spunky and had great storytelling skills, and cooked elaborate meals every day, something totally opposite of her own mom. She had stopped cooking when Britney graduated. Her dad didn't mind. He took over the cooking duties and seemed to enjoy it, Britney (whenever she was home) and himself.

Grandma Trucey was a special woman. Bianca remembered one time she told them about her Great Grandmother watching her own mother get lynched in the South. She said that she made a comment to the Master's wife who had made a subtle pass at her husband. The Master was told about the comment and in a few days she was gone. They came in the middle of the night, busted down the door, ran into the house with rifles and took her. Grandma Trucey's Great Grandfather was shot in the incident because he tried to fight them off. They kept a rifle in front of all of the men in the house and slapped the women and children around until they were in a state of shock. Her Great Grandmother was hung from a tree with her hands placed on a piece of wood cut out to fit them. The screams turned into whimpers and then loud prayers to the man upstairs. When the perpetrators of this despicable, dehumanizing, and barbaric act left, an eerie silence lingered in the air. The family climbed up in the tree and removed her limp body. Amazingly she had a look of serenity on her welted and bruised face. "Great Granddaddy was never the same," said Grandma Trucey.

When she finished the story Bianca was in tears. Mia told her she had been telling that story since they were little. Grandma Trucey always told us to pick and choose when we decided to confront someone. Some things can and should be let go, she would tell us. There was something about the way the older generation told their stories of the past that was so intense.

After Bianca got her record deal she moved out of the house. Everyone was very supportive and happy for her. However, she did miss sitting and talking to Grandma Trucey. "You are still a part of this family," she would always tell Bianca.

Bianca's schedule had gotten so hectic she wasn't able to visit as often as she would have liked. Bianca still, called to say hello. She often asked Grandma Trucey how she remained a size two having had several kids and without ever working out. She now asked Mia how Grandma Trucey was doing.

"I don't know how Grandma stayed so small after all of these years. With age comes weight gain! It is like it goes hand in hand. I don't even want to expound on the age thing."

"Yeah, I feel like we're getting old," said Mia.

"Yeah, a lot of times I feel like that too."

"At least we still have our figures!" Mia remarked.

"If I didn't work out on a regular basis, who knows what my body would look like! I'm short, so I have to watch when and what I eat."

"No you don't. You still eat late at night."

"I don't do it as much!" Bianca tried to sound convincing. They laughed. Chocolate cake had always been her weakness since college. Maria said she was going to make her a low fat, low carbohydrate, minimum sugar cake. Bianca had said that after all of that it would probably taste as nasty as liver! They both laughed. Bianca had to order her assistant, Tanza, Maria, Rocki and security not to make any more cake runs even if she begged, and she has been known to do that! Bianca would joke with them and say she had to be careful not to grow wider width-wise!

Bianca was 5'2 and Mia was 5'5. They were both complementing each other on being natural beauties. Mia attributed her beautiful clear skin to Noxzema. Mia teased Bianca because her hair always looked like she had stepped right out of the hair salon. Bianca would reply, "Technically, I did in my house!" Her stylist Lexi was the best around. She was quick, creative and always had Bianca's hair looking silky even when Bianca first got sick. The stress took her hair out in two sections, the middle, and back. Lexi took Bianca to a weaving manufacturer in Manhattan for a private consultation.   The African woman matched the hair perfectly. It looked so real Bianca couldn't tell where her hair ended and the new hair began.

Although Mia lived in Compton, the women of her family were elegant. Bianca was always trying to get Mia to practice Entertainment Law after graduation. "Are you sure you don't want to go into Entertainment Law?"

"Girl, no. After all of the drama you've been through trying to break in, I don't want any part!"

"But I'm in!" Bianca smiled.

"No thanks.   I'll stick to criminal law.   The entertainment industry is so crooked, I'll probably be convicting some of your friends!" She would say as they laughed.

"Yeah, yeah I know."

Between Mia studying and her career, they hardly spent time together anymore.

Bianca was trying to rest and add normalcy to her life in between gigs, but that seemed difficult to juggle for her. Longevity in the business was tough. Bianca always thanked God for her parents, because, in her opinion, they had raised a self-sufficient, strong, independent, drop-dead gorgeous woman. At least this is what she use to believe, regarding the being gorgeous part anyhow.

She and Mia felt lucky to have each other as friends. They had never had a fight. They had never been mad at each other. They would often joke about how crazy that was because truthfully, in their opinion, women were catty and crazy. If the truth were to be known, both women were a little bourgeoisie at times. This was not because of money, but more because of upbringing and natural spirits. The media always wrote about Bianca's vibrant personality, elegant walk and demeanor. She seemed to glide down the red carpet and onto the stage to receive her awards. One article read, It *doesn't get any better than the beautiful, Bianca Baxter!*

Mia noticed Bianca didn't look so good. She had lost a lot of weight. Her face looked drawn. Mia became serious and asked her if everything was okay. Bianca didn't want to talk at length about her situation. She had kept her secret for so long.

Bianca looked sad and weary. Her beautiful almond shaped eyes were hollow, almost the same as a person that had been up all night crying or driving a long distance with no rest in sight. Her weight had dropped to what Mia reminded her was an unnatural size. Her skin didn't have its natural glow. Her hair did not flow as usual. Bianca's Doctor told her that no matter how much money she spent on her medications domestically and internationally, if she didn't get plenty of rest and maintain a healthful diet, her beautiful appearance would be compromised. Therefore no stress was allowed. It was noticeable to Mia but not as noticeable to the public yet. Bianca knew she had better start taking better care of herself. Otherwise it would show.

This meant she had to stop fighting with Ricky, her staff and the world-renowned physical trainer, Edward Banker.

Lately Bianca had been fighting with him because she was constantly in slack mode. Her workout consisted of a 5:00 a.m. daily hard-core workout for two hours except when she was on set or in the studio. Then it was crazy hours such as 1:00 a.m., 11:00 a.m. or 7:00 p.m. Circuit training was the best type of workout. Edward had Bianca start with stretching, a 10 minute warm up run through the hills on her property. They would then go back to her home gym and she would do the bike for 10 minutes, lift weights for five, jump rope for 10, crunches on the ball for five, climb the stair machine for five, pilates for 10, and crunches on the floor for five. She would repeat the exercises in various orders, which at first made the art of working out a pleasure.

Bianca continued to lie to Mia about her deteriorating looks. However, she was burnt out from working and traveling so much. Mia changed the subject and asked how Ricky was doing. Bianca's entire disposition changed from chipper to one with a chip on their shoulder. She dreaded telling Mia they had broken up.

"Again?" Mia didn't seem to take Bianca seriously until she looked at her face. "Girl, I'm sorry. Retract that statement. When did you two break up? You didn't tell me. I mean, I know we don't see each other as much as we use to but we still talk on the phone, we're always sending emails."

"I know. I was going to tell you but I've been struggling with it myself. It happened a few weeks ago. It is really hard to sever our relationship because he signed me to the label, and no matter what, I'm his protégé." Bianca knew that as long as she stayed with Millennium, Ricky would be involved in her life. Her mind drifted to the good times she and Ricky had shared.

She remembered him being respectful of her time and schedule. He was genuine. He was her protector in the music industry. He and her manager would go at it sometimes because Ricky had huge plans for her. On Friday nights they played cards, cut out articles about Bianca and some about him. Bianca had a $20,000 voice activated system installed into her home entertainment center. She would sit on her white leather sofa and tell the system to play BET, then tell it to play MTV, then VH1, while she and Ricky cuddled. Bianca always criticized her videos. Ricky would tell her she was bugging because she was a trendsetting superstar in the making, and she held onto his every word.

Aside from her family and best friend, he was her biggest most dedicated fan. They went everywhere and did everything together. One time they were at one of Hollywood's highest profile restaurants, and as they were exiting the Moroccan-decorated venue, a reporter began taking tons of pictures, while bombarding her with questions. Bianca was tired and Ricky wasn't having it. He warned the reporter twice before he snatched the camera with his left hand and used his right hand to deliver the most fierce, karate, open handed slap, anyone had ever seen. As he politely handed him back his camera, moved close to the reporter, then spat right in his face. The irate reporter filed a lawsuit, which was thrown out due to lack of evidence. Strangely, not one member of the large crowd neither saw nor heard anything. Bianca, who avoided negative press like the plague, made Ricky promise to never do that again unless their lives were truly in danger.

The first time Bianca and Ricky made love was indeed the most beautiful experience she had ever encountered of her life. They had gone to Aruba to relax and had rented a house on the beach. They made love to the sound of the ocean ringing in their ears. They rode around the island in golf carts at dusk and made love when the sun went down all over the island. Bianca loved the island so much, she purchased a five bedroom pink stucco home several years later. Her brothers loved Ricky and thought he was cool. They all had great conversation. If only she could go back into the past, she would be so much happier, she thought. In reality, everything done in the past becomes etched in stone.

Bianca was still hungry. She pressed a button to ask Rocki to bring her some smoked salmon and crackers, which had been left over from the morning.

"Bianca, I'm so sorry about you and Ricky." Mia got up to hug her. Bianca missed her best friend. At that very moment she felt 75 percent better. Her old spunky demeanor returned, as she reverted back to her old beliefs. Time heals all wounds. She explained to Mia about the nasty email and how she fixed her computer so he couldn't reply. They both laughed. Bianca was born to be a songwriter and Mia knew it, for she had made a substantial living publishing hits for herself and others. Mia knew the email probably messed with Ricky's head and though curious, she was reluctant to ask what had been said. Bianca laughed mischievously. Bianca told Mia that she said some mess about how foul and how much of a womanizer he was. Mia told Bianca that sexual comments really hit brothers where it hurt. Bianca then classified men as being egotistical frick heads! She was proud of her letter. Both women laughed uncontrollably.

Rocki and Marie put more salad and salmon on Bianca and Mia's plate, then Rocki poured fresh lemonade into matching tall thin aqua-colored glasses.

Mia knew Bianca was fed up with her relationship with Ricky, and Bianca knew Mia understood he had deserved it for all of the drama he had put her through. Mia couldn't stop laughing as she wiped the tears from her eyes. Mia made reference to nothing having changed with Bianca since college, except that now, she was rich and pampered. A long discussion of screwing became the topic of conversation.

In college, Bianca would hold the sex from guys for years. Then she would get mad if and when they screwed someone else. She seriously felt if the relationship was strong enough they should wait. Her girlfriends would tease her by asking her what the heck she was waiting for, the turn of the century! At that time, Bianca had every intention of waiting until marriage.

Both women joked around and laughed about how their personalities were in college and shortly afterwards. Although it had been many years ago, it felt like yesterday. Bianca jokingly told Mia that if she continued teasing her about her sexually holding out days, it might be the icebreaker that determined just how mad she would become at her. Bianca laughed as she gently pushed Mia's arm. Supreme Baxter had always taught her girls, Bianca, Delaney and Britney that sex should be special and something that should be reserved for the right person. Eric had been Delaney's first. She met him in college and later they were married. Bianca remembered the night it happened. She and Mia were clubbing when Delaney left her a message on her cell phone at midnight PST, from Eric's bathroom. The funny part was when Bianca called her back, Delaney was whispering. Bianca and Mia were very drunk, so to them, everything was funny.

You screwed him! Bianca had yelled out in the middle of the club. It was simultaneous to the DJ transitioning to a slow song, so the music was not as loud. Everyone in the bar zoomed in on Bianca's conversation. Mia thought it was hilarious. Guys from UCLA and the neighborhood walked over to them wanting to know who screwed who because they wanted to screw them! Hearing the input from strangers made Delaney mad and she hung up. Bianca tried to feel bad but was way too intoxicated. Mia was banging on the table from laughter. She had always felt Bianca was private and she'd never heard her discuss sex so openly.

"When you first told me that you had to be married to do it, I thought to myself, *she is crazy.*"

"Later for you! You and I both can't even count the brothers you slept with, on both of our hands and toes! I keep telling you to get that videotape 'Too Much Meaningless Sex Lies Heavy on the Soul' by Minister, Mable Kira. Lots of brothers have been between your sheets!"

"It was ALL good! Well, with the exception of a few!" Mia looked up reminiscing in her mind, and laughed again. Bianca joined her friend in the laughter.

"You're nuts," said Bianca.

"Girl, I have stories to tell my children."

"If they don't read about it first!" Said Bianca.

"What about Britney? I don't think she listened to your mom."

"Girl, please, I think she came out of her womb looking for the male species!"

"I know your fine brothers weren't trying to hear that nonsense about holding out."

"Heck no, but I must say, they are good men. They have grown into being nice, responsible men."

"That's what you think."

"What is that suppose to mean?" Bianca looked a little confused.

"I have a confession to make."

"What?"

"Remember when Armani came to visit you when you were living with Trish, Leah, Cristy, and Charmaine?"

"Which time? He came several times."

"The first time?"

"Yeahhhhhh."

Bianca looked at Mia inquisitively.

"Remember when I told you I couldn't go out because at the last minute I had to meet with someone in my study group?"

"Yeah," said Bianca.

"I hooked up with your brother."

"No, you didn't."

Bianca stared at Mia in disbelief. "What? Where did you all go? Bianca sounded like a country parent from rural America.

"We went to Roscoe's Chicken and Waffle and then to my house. Remember Mom and Grandma went away for the weekend to visit Grandma's sister Lena?"

"Yeah." Bianca was puzzled.

"Well...."

"I don't want to hear anymore. I remember the night he told me he was going to stay at his friend Reggie's because they were going to hang out late."

"They did during the day! I know we never had any secrets but I couldn't tell you your brother flipped me!"

"Yuk. I can't listen to this," Bianca frowned with disgust.

Mia nervously laughed.

"I can't imagine my baby brother." Bianca was repulsed.

"Girl, he wasn't a baby!"

"Hey, hey, that's enough. Can we change the subject, ho?" Bianca laughed and looked at Mia in disbelief.

"I cannot believe you both kept this from me for all of these years."

"I wasn't sure if you would be mad at me."

"I am mad at you!" Bianca mushed her in the forehead with her two fingers. "You didn't think about it too hard, you still did it. You stank heifer!"

"Should I say it was a situation that just happened?" They laughed.

"Yeah, right. You just happened to have your legs wide open while my brother was butt naked in the same room!" Said Bianca.

Mia laughed.

"Yuk. I'm shocked," Bianca said to Mia laughing. "I can't entertain this conversation. Can we change the subject, nasty girl?"

"Okay, what do you want to talk about?"

"What I should do about my man? I mean my ex-man!" Bianca immediately caught her choice of words.

"What do you mean?"

"I mean, I really care about Ricky but I feel like I'm stuck with him." Bianca felt stuck because who would want a person with her condition, she thought. Who would love her? She needed and enjoyed companionship.

"Bianca, you should never feel stuck with anyone." Had Mia known the entire story she would understand Bianca's point of view.

Bianca caught herself inside her thoughts as she altered the direction of the conversation. "I'm not trying to get dogged any more than I already have."

"Bianca, live a little. You always worry about getting dogged. You have never really experienced getting dogged, so what is the problem? It's negative thinking. Take your own advice about enjoying this big world and go with the flow. Life is about taking chances. He's not dogging you and if he does, you're strong. Move on."

The words *move on* rang loud in Bianca's ears. How could she have gotten herself into her current situation? How would she get out? Dying slowly is devastating to the mind and spirit. Bianca and Mia were so close, with the exception of this one little secret.

"Let your relationship with Ricky be a learning experience and grow from it. Now shut the hell up. You are so dramatic," said Mia.

"Gee, thanks for caring."

"You know I'm kidding. But you are dramatic."

"I know. I can't help it."

"I see where Britney gets her drama from!"

"She is worse. She is the real drama queen!" Bianca and Mia laughed.

"Seriously, are you okay with your situation with Ricky?"

"No, but I will be in, eternal time."

"What?" Mia curiously looked at Bianca.

"It felt so right when I first slept with him. I never felt that way before. Maybe I'm whipped," she half lied. Ricky was great in bed. However, if she wasn't ill she would have gone on a quest to locate another great guy in bed. "He screws me like I have never been screwed before. No one has ever made me scream so loud. The people in San Francisco could hear me! I almost want to host a banquet in his honor, put up flyers around the city, and put an ad in the newspaper...."

Mia interrupted Bianca before she could finish her speech. "Girl, stop it," she said laughing so hard she had a stream of tears flowing down her face. "Look, if it felt right, then it was right, especially for you, because you never gave it up that easily. Try following your heart sometimes. It's not a bad thing you know. Okay, maybe you're going through some hard times, but that is what relationships are all about. You know I have had my problems with Thomas." Bianca flashed back to the days when Thomas, Mia's boyfriend wasn't acting right.

Thomas had allegedly gotten his ex-girlfriend pregnant while dating Mia. The stuff hit the roof. According to the ex-girlfriend, she never left the picture. They later found out that he was still sleeping with her and without a condom. She suspected something because for months he had been acting nervous about something. One night he said that he was out with one of his boys and didn't tell his boy. The friend called to see if Thomas was home and of course Mia, being a woman, played along with the phone call. That night she confronted Thomas with a skillet.

She had paged Thomas and told him he needed to get home ASAP. She had called Bianca and told her about the mess. Bianca felt it was time for her to break up with him, but didn't know how to tell Mia because in Mia's eyes Thomas was going to be her husband. This was a test of their friendship. Bianca decided to stay close by prepared to catch Mia when and if she fell. After all, he wasn't beating her. Mia phoned Bianca and told her she would call her back within the hour. She had been crying uncontrollably and screaming at the top of her lungs. Bianca's heart bled for her. She had never heard Mia sound so devastated. She hated Thomas for doing this to her best friend. She extended a helping hand but Mia insisted she would be okay and would call back. She had hung up before Bianca could say anything else. When several hours-lapsed, Bianca called Thomas's house, Mia's house, her cell phone, and got voice mails on all three. Mia called Bianca at three a.m. from a pay phone in downtown Los Angeles. Bianca hadn't been fully asleep because she had been so worried. Mia sounded so scorned. Bianca immediately sat up in her bed.

Bianca asked her if Thomas had hurt her. Mia replied, "only emotionally." Bianca asked where he was. Mia said she didn't know, but she had hit him really hard, saw blood, ran out of the house, jumped in her car, and drove as fast as she could. She had reached for her cell phone and realized she had left it in his house. Mia was breathing heavily and sounded hyped. Almost like a crackhead that had just gotten hooked up.

Bianca drove to where Mia was, told her to drive slowly, with her hazard lights on, while she followed closely behind her. Bianca had her servants lay out a matching washcloth and towel set and pajamas by the time they arrived at her house. While Mia was in the shower, Bianca called her assistant and canceled her appointments for the next day. The servant made them a large pot of herbal relaxation tea, which Bianca had shipped every month from Egypt. They sipped their refreshing tea and laid in the powder blue loft bedroom, on two separate four-foot high, super king sized, solid oak wood beds, with fluffy pillows and blankets, while they talked until the sun was beaming through the 12 foot windows.

Mia told Bianca that forty-five minutes after Thomas was supposedly on his way home, the ex called and told her everything. She said Thomas had just left and she and he had been sleeping together off and on since he and Mia met. Mia wasn't clear on her exact words. According to the ex, they were trying to work out their differences and she was now six weeks pregnant. Mia cried so hard, it made Bianca cry. Her hands were trembling as she tried to control her pouring tears. Bianca pressed the intercom for her servant to bring a box of tissue and some more tea. Bianca went over and gave her a big hug.

Apparently when confronted, Thomas had been shocked and began to stutter. That made Mia livid. That's why she said she hit him. They split up for a year and a half and Mia was the epitome of a miserable, bitter woman. She gained thirty pounds. Soon after the ordeal her grades in law school suffered. She tried to date other guys but said it was not the same, so she stopped dating altogether. Her mom, grandmother, and Bianca were worried. Mia took a year off from school and went on the road with Bianca for a little while, but said she couldn't deal with all of the phonies, drugs and sex going on.

Mia decided to take a weekend trip to Barbados, alone. She said when she returned she would start putting meaning back into her life. Bianca was happy about her decision. When Mia returned she enrolled in school, got her grades back on track, and began putting her life back together again. She had been single for well over a year until she let Thomas back into her life.

Out of the blue, Mia called Bianca one day, and asked her how she would feel if she went on a date with Thomas. "Thomas, now there's a blast from the past," Bianca answered.

She told her she had run into his mom, who had said he was still single and always talked about her. She told Mia that the ex had lied and wasn't pregnant after all. Mia told Thomas' mom, her son had told her that as well, but that she was too hurt to believe him. The pregnancy may not have been true, but the fact that he was sleeping with her was way too much for her heart and mind to bear. Thomas' mom told Mia she had been right, and had every reason not to take him back. She made Mia swear if she ever spoke with Thomas again, she didn't hear the story from her but asked Mia to *just talk to him*. By the time Mia had gotten home Thomas had left her two messages. The first message was, *Hi Mia, its Thomas. I know it has been a while. My mom said she saw you today and you asked her to tell me to call you. I guess you're not back from shopping yet. I have moved and have a new phone number. Call me at your earliest convenience. Take care.* That was the macho message. Then there was a second message. It sounded less macho and contained a little bit of desperation to get her to respond. *Hey Mia, it's Thomas again. I guess you haven't made it back home yet. You always did like to shop, he nervously laughed. Call me as soon as you get in. It doesn't matter if it's four a.m.*

Mia called Bianca first to let her listen to his messages. "Do you think I should call him?"

"Do you want to call him?" Bianca asked.

"Honestly?"

"Honestly." Bianca said.

"Yes, I really miss him."

"Well, you have your answer."

She called and the rest is history. They went on a beautiful date and have been together since. They worked out the situation with the ex. Thomas told her he had slept with her twice while he and Mia were together. One of those two times, he didn't use a condom. He felt terrible. The ex kept calling him at home, his job, his cell, and his mom's house. He told her several times it was over. He hadn't told Mia because he thought, as a man, he could handle it. Mia didn't believe him but she wanted him back. She knew in her heart he loved her and was truly sorry.

Mia told Bianca Thomas had broken down in tears. She said she had never seen him cry before, and that in itself, had made her cry. It suddenly occurred to both of them, they must have looked like two fools crying in public!

"You have to take the good with the bad. Love is beautiful," said Mia.

"Yeah, when it is reciprocated," said Bianca.

"What makes you think it isn't being reciprocated? Men are stupid sometimes. You have to show them how to treat you. The key is to make them think they are in control. Bianca stop sabotaging and jinxing your relationship."

"I think I'm scared." Bianca's eyes watered. With all of her might, she could not hold back her long overdue tears. "It's really hard being me." She got up to get a tissue. "I have a great deal of pressure inside of me. There are certain things in my life that I didn't ask for nor did I foresee." She was fidgeting. "If I had to do it all over again, I would give up everything to be whole again."

"You are whole. You're going through a storm right now and it is okay." Mia kneeled down in front of Bianca. Bianca delved into the actress side of herself to conjure up her calm side. The last thing she wanted was for her secret to be out even if it was with someone she fully trusted.

"It's all right. It's normal. Just learn to relax. You have been with Ricky for a long time. Why are you all of a sudden scared?"

"Things have happened between us and I don't think I can ever fully recover."

"I recovered from my situation with Thomas." Bianca almost lost her composure again. However, she knew Mia didn't fully understand.

"Whatever it is, you two can work through it."

"You don't understand," said Bianca.

"I do. Remember, I have been through it." *She doesn't know the whole story*, flashed through Bianca's head. She again, tried to control her saddened emotions.

"Do you want some wine?" The servant came in the kitchen and asked.

"Sure," said both women. Suddenly the doorbell rang. Everyone looked up at the intercom.

"Who the heck is at my door?" Bianca angrily said.

"I'll get it, madam."

"No, I'll answer it. I forgot to let security know he is no longer welcome here. Thanks."

The doorbell rang again. Bianca stood up and marched to the front door.

CHAPTER 9
DEEP THOUGHTS
RICKY

Involved in heavy thoughts, Ricky passed right by the long driveway leading to Bianca's house and was headed towards the back of the estate. He put the car in reverse and drove up to security.

"Hey Ricky," said the tall, dark-haired security guard. "I haven't seen you in a few weeks."

"Hey man. I've been traveling." Ricky was hoping Bianca didn't tell him they had broken up. He gave a sigh of relief as the gate was lifted.

"Take care buddy," said the security guard.

"Okay," said Ricky as he drove the half-mile to get to Bianca's circular driveway.

He quickly reverted back to his Brooklyn years and started to feel sad again. He wished he could speak with his boys to get some quick advice.

Suddenly he had butterflies in his stomach. His nerves were shot. He wasn't close enough with anyone to tell them how he felt. He considered Scooter, but Scooter always threw stupid other women up in his face. He didn't always want to hear that.

Ricky hardly ever spoke to his mom. She was always too busy trying to locate his stepfather's whereabouts. If he wasn't chasing the women in the neighborhood, he was out getting drunk at the local bar/restaurant/poolroom. Ricky never met his own father. Every time he asked his mom where he was, she would say she didn't know. He often wanted to ask her, how she could lay down with a man, have a child, and not care about him or his whereabouts? At least for the sake of the child, Ricky wondered what his personality was like, what his father looked like, what were his likes and dislikes. After a while, Ricky stopped asking about him. He figured if he wanted to find him, he would. Ricky would sit in his room and think about how he hadn't asked to be born, but shit since he was, he had the right to feel accepted. Over the years, his anger made him only want to see the idiot so he could beat his ass for his contribution to his existence. Warren's dad was like a father to Ricky. When they went out, people thought they were all family. Warren's parents had Warren when they were fifteen, then had three other girls much later on.

Ricky wished his mom had had more children. Then again, maybe it was best she didn't. She wouldn't have paid much attention to them either.

Ricky parked his truck and got out. He walked up to the door and rang the bell while still somewhat thinking of thoughts about old times.

"Excuse me. Why are you here?" Bianca asked.

His thoughts were suddenly interrupted. Bianca was standing in the doorway looking at him like he must have lost his mind.

"We need to talk." Ricky stumbled with his words like a sucker! "Are you going to let me in?"

"Let you in for what?" Bianca asked.

"Would you rather we talk outside?"

"I'd rather not talk at all."

"Bianca, stop it. This isn't easy for me either. Let me come in. I need to talk to you."

Bianca stepped to the side. Ricky walked into one of the living rooms and sat down on her crème colored suede couch. She shut the door and followed. Mia walked out of the kitchen.

"Hey lady, how are you?" Ricky asked.

"Hey Ricky, I'm fine. I was just leaving."

"No, you weren't," said Bianca sternly.

"I didn't know you were here," said Ricky.

"You didn't ask, snapped Bianca. Mia, you don't have to leave."

"That's okay. I didn't want to stay long. I just wanted to come by and see you.
My sweetie is meeting me at my house. He said he wants to show me something
regarding my taxes."

"Are you sure?" asked Bianca, as she looked scathingly at Ricky.

"Yes, plus I think you two need to talk." Mia grabbed her purse and keys.

"Thanks for lunch. It was great." Bianca walked over and gave Mia a hug. Mia whispered to her. "If you need me, page me. I'll be at the library later on today as well as all day tomorrow."

"What makes you think he is going to be here all night?"

"I didn't say it. You did! Girl, just call me if you need me."

Bianca walked Mia to the door. Ricky grabbed the remote and turned on the big-screen television as Bianca and Mia hugged again.

"Be strong, girl, and lighten up a little," said Mia. "Make-up sex is the best sex by far!"

"I can't continue to allow him to cheat on me and disrespect me."

"Talk to him straight up. Tell him how you feel. Be very specific and clear," Mia whispered.

"You just don't know the half," Bianca whispered.

"We never do." Mia dismissed Bianca's comment. "Try not to stress. It's going to be okay. Stay strong and focus on your career."

"I will. Take care and I'll speak to you this week. Say hello to Thomas for me." "I will. I love you, best friend."

"Me too," said Bianca.

Bianca shut the door and walked to the other side of the 1,000 square foot room from where Ricky was sitting, and sat down on one of her love seats. "You have ten minutes to say whatever it is you have to say. Then you have to get out. Now start talking."

"Damn," Ricky tried not to have an attitude.

CHAPTER 10
REPEAT
BIANCA

As Bianca stared at him, Ricky thought he'd better hurry up and say whatever it was he had to say so he could exit rather quickly! He went off on a tangent about the email that she sent. After about a minute she stopped him.

"Look, it's how I feel. I'm tired of your mess. I'm tired of arguing with you. My family is sick of me complaining and it's starting to show on my face. We're both sick because of your selfish actions. It's not the other way around. I'm scared. I'm dying a slow death and you're still running around chasing women. What the heck is wrong with you? What the hell is wrong with me?" Bianca realized she too must have a problem because she had stayed in this dysfunctional relationship, knowing the circumstances. "I have already allowed you to take away my self-esteem. I can't bring a child into this world knowing I am sick. I can't afford to lose any more weight. You're insensitive and an egotistical piece of pure fresh laid shit. Sometimes I feel like killing you."

Ricky humbly interrupted. "What? I love you, Bianca. I don't want to fight with you."

"Ricky, you are stressing me out and you are too much drama."

"You're the one with the drama, and you are too jealous and insecure." Ricky knew he probably should not have said that.

"Too insecure and jealous?" she screamed. "I didn't have an insecure bone in my body until I met your sorry behind. I resent the fact that you would allow those words to come out of your mouth. You have lost your damn mind!" Bianca jumped up out of her seat, fuming. "Get the hell out," she screamed. "I don't need this."

"Madam, is everything okay?" asked Arthur, one of Bianca's British servants, as he returned from taking the trash outside. "Shall I call security?"

"B, please don't let him call security."

"No, Arthur, we'll be fine. Everything is okay."

"Let me know if you need anything, madam." His eyes pierced through Ricky's soul.

Ricky disregarded Bianca's harsh words. He also dismissed Arthur's sharp stare. He knew Arthur didn't like him ever since his last argument with Bianca. "Bianca, I love you. I want to be with you. Why are you always bugging? I can never please you. Nothing is ever good enough for you."

"Ricky, the fact that I find phone numbers in your pockets and in your house, on paper napkins, is a problem. Girls whom I don't know call your house and hang up on me."

He walked around the room. "B, I work in the same industry as you. People of the opposite sex are going to call."

"Who's Simone?" Bianca asked.

"Who?" Ricky looked a little shady.

"Rocky was doing our laundry and found her number on a napkin. Do you remember you bastard?"

"I told you then and I'm telling you now, I don't know any Simone. I don't know how that number got in my pocket." Ricky looked away from Bianca.

"You are a damn liar. I don't believe you. Shall we call her?"

"Call her." Ricky sounded pissed off.

Bianca knew the truth would hurt badly, but she was tired of dealing with unfaithfulness. Besides, nothing could be more traumatic than finding out she had a disease. He didn't even have the decency to alarm her. A few years ago, while on tour, she had been feeling fatigued for months, and couldn't seem to kick a draining cold, plus she had a painful sore throat. She contacted her doctor while in Cleveland, Ohio and informed him of her symptoms. He met her in Milwaukee, the next city on her itinerary, and thoroughly discussed her symptoms and examined her. He asked her if she had ever had an AIDS test. She didn't think there was a reason to. He suggested that she have one and she confidently obliged.

A week passed. While back in California for a day, she received a call from her doctor. When Doctor John Bellman told her she had AIDS, she screamed so loud all twelve of her staff members came running out to her pool where she had been relaxing. Bianca not wanting to divulge her huge secret dismissed the entire staff for two weeks. She made sure they unplugged all 60 phones in the house prior to their departure. She had her assistant cancel all appointments including her tour, guest appearances, interviews, and charity events. She informed security to not allow any visitors on the property. She stayed in bed and cried every day. She eventually contacted her doctor, and finally allowed him to visit. He was the one that brought her spirits back after she'd gone over to Ricky's house, and beat the crap out of him until the police were called. She left before they arrived and Ricky covered for her. Later, she refused to talk to him. He left her several letters at the security desk saying how sorry he was and how much he truly loved her.

Bianca knew she had to get Ricky out of her system. When they finally made up he promised her he would be faithful and fully commit himself to solely her. He would be with her for the rest of her life. Now she was faced with having to deal with yet another woman. She wanted to face this head on.

"You can call the number if you want to."

Bianca called Rocki on the intercom and asked her to bring her the napkin she had been asked to put in a safe place. Ricky was trying to look confident as she dialed the number on speakerphone. After three rings, Simone's machine picked up.

"You have reached 213-555-5555, we're either unavailable or screening our calls! Press 1 for Simone, 2 for Trisha, or 3 for both of us."

Bianca pressed '1'.

"What are you doing?" said Ricky looking nervous.

"Don't worry about it," said Bianca trying to hold her composure so she wouldn't go ballistic on him again.

"Hey, how are you?" Bianca froze. *"Psych, I will not be available to answer your call until May 1st. If this call is urgent, I can be reached in the Mardi Gras town for Jazz Fest.*

The number is: 504-555-1212, room number: 513, or try my cell at 818-555-6753."

Bianca hung up feeling relieved. "So your secret chick is in New Orleans for a little while, huh?"

"There you go with that insecure bullshit again. Bianca, look I don't want to fight anymore. If you want to break up with me, fuck it, do it and stick with the decision."

"Don't try that psychology mess with me. It's not working. You rang my doorbell. You are the one that has the womanizing problem. We have been together for years. It's no secret why we break up. You can't keep your thing on lock down."

"You..." Ricky attempted to respond to Bianca.

"Shut up! I'm not finished talking."

"Bianca, I'm not going to continue to allow you to talk to me like I'm a pile of shit."

"Why, Ricky? You treat me like shit."

"I do not!"

"I said I'm not finished. You said you wanted to talk. I listened and now I'm talking. Try being a good listener. You have slept with so many girls, it's sickening. What makes you think a woman wants to marry a sleazy man?" Bianca frowned causing her forehead to wrinkle.

"What are you talking about?" Ricky looked puzzled.

"A woman doesn't want to marry a guy that has slept with every girl he comes in contact with," said Bianca.

"I have not slept with every girl that I have come in contact with."

"Then why do girls call your house and ask me who I am? Why do I get lots of hang-ups? Why does your pager and cell phone ring all night? Why do I have to tell you to turn the shit off? Why are girls calling and saying they slept with you and they are not the only ones you are screwing? Why, when I was at your house and checked your messages, did some girl named Cheryl call asking you where you were? She said she called your cell and paged you. She also said she couldn't leave the clinic without an escort because they had given her a local anesthesia for the abortion. Other girls have called. Who are

Beverly, Tiny, and Nicole? I am surprised no one has sued you. If anyone finds out about my sickness, damn you, I will see to it that you're destroyed." Bianca was screaming and trying to fight back her uncontrolled tears.

"Madam, is everything okay?" Arthur asked through the intercom.

"I'm fine. Stop asking me," Bianca snapped.

"Sorry to bother you madam." His voice faded.

"Bianca, please stop crying." Ricky walked over to her.

"Get the hell away from me," she yelled.

Ricky fearfully stopped dead in his tracks.

"I know you've only seen me act like this, one other time, of which we will not discuss, because I might lose it." Her voice was low and direct while her eyes cut into him.

Ricky turned around with his head down and walked back over to the couch and sat down. He ran his hands through his curly hair.

"How could you continue to disrespect me like you do? Damn it, look at me when I'm talking to you. I'm not one of your dumb artists or funky little tramps."

Ricky lifted his head and looked at Bianca with a serious face.

"B, you are really losing it. First of all, you should not have been checking my answering machine. Those messages were not for you. They were for me."

"Is that all you have to say to me? Don't you tell me what I should and should not have done. We should end this discussion right now because you are really pissing me off."

Bianca got up to get a Kleenex from the downstairs bathroom. While there she glanced in the mirror. *"God help me. I'm a mess,"* she mumbled while blotting her red, puffy eyes with a cold washcloth before going back upstairs.

A few minutes later Bianca was sitting on her loveseat staring at Ricky with sadness in her eyes and thinking about how she had even surprised herself with her uncanny behavior.

"Bianca, you are pissing yourself off," Ricky said in a calm voice. "You are stressing over nothing. I love you so much."

"Shut the hell up. I'm sick of trying to mend this relationship. You are affecting my life. I'm sick of you trying to make me feel like I'm the one with the problem."

"Bianca, I don't make you feel that way. You are paranoid."

"I'm paranoid? Are you saying you never cheated on me?" She began to cry again. This time her bottom lip trembled uncontrollably.

"I have never cheated on you." Ricky looked towards the floor.

"Look at me in my face and say that, you lying bastard."

Ricky stared into Bianca's eyes. "Look, I did cheat once and we discussed it. I promised I would never do it again and now I feel like you accuse me of cheating whenever something doesn't seem right to you. I don't know how to show you that I love you any more than I have." Ricky's sincere apology showed through his lovesick eyes.

"Being a great screw is not showing me you love me. Any man can do that. I'm a celebrity. I could have had any man I wanted. You stopped that. If you wanted to be with lots of women, you should have told me. You should have told me more about your past. That would have given me other options."

"You're right. I should have told you I was sick. B, before you, I never loved or trusted any woman. When I fell in love with you I couldn't tell you. I was scared of dying but more importantly, I was afraid of losing you, and that is the honest truth. Woman, I really do love you but you are draining me too. What do you want me to do?"

"Be honest."

"I have tried to be honest. I love you."

"I love you, too," Bianca said in between whimpers, "but this relationship is destroying me." She continued to wipe her face with the balled-up, wet Kleenex then made her third trip to the bathroom for more. This time she also blew her nose and felt a strong headache coming on. Making her way back into her living room, Bianca couldn't help but still look at Ricky with disgust.

"What can I do to show you I have changed? Listen, I know I caused your sickness and for that I am truly sorry. Really, I am but I don't want to break up. I want to be with you," said Ricky.

"I don't know but everything is so different now. What happened to the wonderful man that use to always wish for my days to be joyous? What happened to the man that said, meet me at the security desk with nothing but the clothes on my back? We flew to Hawaii for a few days. The man that had a BMW truck delivered to the recording studio when we first met. The man who gloated over me, even when I looked and felt busted beyond repair."

"Baby, I'm still here."

"If we are going to be together, we have to go to therapy."

"Therapy! I don't I need no damn therapy. Black people don't get therapy. I'm not crazy."

"Ricky, I'm not saying you are crazy, but I think you have some issues that need to be addressed and resolved. Therapy is not a black or white issue. We need to meet with someone unfamiliar to us. I don't have the inner strength to continue to deal with this. I have some anger and resentment towards you that also needs to be addressed."

"Look, therapy is not for me."

"See Ricky, you are too selfish. You could at least say that you'll think about it."

"Okay B, I will think about it."

"Ricky, just try – that's all I have ever asked of you."

"I want this to work. I love you with all of my heart. I don't want us to have any more blowups like this. You don't look so good. Before you say anything..." Ricky tried to retract the tone of his statement. "I'm truly sorry that I hurt you. That has never been my intentions. I want good things for you. You are a wonderful loyal person and I'm grateful for having you in my camp. I don't want to yell and scream anymore B, I'm getting a headache. Can I sit next to you?" Ricky was a little hesitant but got up anyway and slowly walked over to sit next to Bianca.

"Can I get a kiss?" He said as he looked into her bloodshot red puffy eyes.

"No, I don't feel like kissing," she snapped in a low toned voice.

"Please B. I think we will both feel better."

"I don't care how you feel. This is not about you anymore," said Bianca sounding annoyed.

Ricky ignored her bitter comment. "Baby, can we make up? Can I have a kiss, pleasssssssssssse? Just a small one," he begged as he got closer. "Can I get a smile? I hate seeing you like this."

"Then don't lie to me."

"I never will. Kiss me."

Before Bianca could protest any longer, Ricky leaned in and kissed her on the lips. She responded, but only a little.

"That's all I get? After six years, can a brother get a kiss like you mean it?" he asked in an unintentionally sexy voice.

"Right now, I'm not so sure I can mean it." Bianca said giving him a dry uncommitted quick peck.

"I know you can do better than that."

Bianca leaned over and gave Ricky a meaningful kiss. He then pulled her down on top of him and she responded one hundred percent. He began tickling her.

"Stop it Ricky," she said squirming and slightly giggling.

"Now promise me you will act right."

They were flirting with each other.

"I promise," said Bianca.

"You sound unsure."

"I promise, darn it!" Said Bianca.

"I can't hear you." He tickled her harder.

"Okay, I promise," said Bianca turning her giggles into laughter.

"Say you love me."

"I love you."

"Say it louder."

"Okay, I love you, damnit," Bianca said louder thinking her staff must think she was crazy. She went from screaming to laughing all in approximately an hour.

"Are you swearing?" Ricky asked, laughing.

"No, I'm not swear.... Ricky please s-t-o-p." She was squirming all over the couch bending up and down trying to get away from his hands. "You are going to make me..." She rolled over and fell onto the floor. They were both laughing. Bianca got up and put her palm on his forehead. "I can't believe you. You are crazy."

"Would you like an instant replay?" Ricky laughed and acted like he was going to tickle her again.

"No. I've had enough."

"I really do love your spoiled behind."

"I'm not going to respond to that," she said smiling and for a half of a second forgetting about her sickness and the physical, emotional, and mental pain she had gone through because of it.

CHAPTER 11
LET'S DO IT AGAIN
BIANCA

"Do you want a glass of wine? Mia and I were getting ready to have some wine when you knocked on the door and crashed our little party."

"Woman, you know I don't want any wine! I'll take a beer."

Bianca got up, walked into the kitchen and pulled a crystal wineglass from the shellacked oak wood cabinet and grabbed a bottle from the wine rack. She then grabbed two beers. As she poured the wine into the glass, she thought of Ricky. *Hopefully he'll agree to therapy. Parents can really screw kids up. I'm thankful for my parents.*

"Honey, are you okay in there?" Ricky got up and walked into the kitchen. "Let me help you. I'll carry the beer." *He can be so sweet whenever he wants to, she thought.*

Bianca and Ricky walked back into the living room, Bianca holding the wineglass in her hand. They both sat on the couch. Bianca pressed the remote for the CD player to come on. She pressed track #9. "Suddenly Weeping" came on in the background.

"Sing it Laddy," Bianca said in a low voice.

"I love this song." She closed her eyes to briefly absorb the lyrics.

"Let's make a toast," said Ricky.

They toasted to good times in the future.

"Ricky, don't hurt me anymore."

"I'm not. I'm sorry, Bianca. Can I have a real kiss now?" Ricky said trying to break up the thick cloud of pressure in the room.

Bianca kissed him and felt her body jerk from the warmth of his touch and the hopeful conquering of his respect and heart.

"Please God make him act right," Bianca quietly said to herself.

"What did you say?" Ricky looked at her inquisitively.

"Nothing. Just having a moment with God," Bianca suddenly felt a sense of peace for now.

Ricky smiled. "Do you need me to step out of the room for a few minutes?" he asked jokingly.

"No, I'm done."

Ricky stared at Bianca. "Are you sure?" He fondly smiled.

"Yes Ricky, I'm fine, she whispered." Her eyes were low and the wine buzz had definitely kicked in. They kissed and held each other like newlyweds.

"Let's get in the Jacuzzi," whispered Ricky in a monotone voice.

"Okay, in a minute. Just hold me. I want to enjoy you." For the first time in weeks Bianca felt like she could sleep through the night.

"Why? Do you think I'm going somewhere?" He squeezed her tighter.

"One can never tell when it comes to you, Ricky."

"You are the one who is always breaking up with me." Bianca lifted her head. "You make me break up with you," she whispered.

Ricky gently pulled her head back down on his shoulders. "Shhh, let's enjoy each other."

"If you want us to enjoy each other, then show me without hurting me."

"I'm trying to show you now if you'll just chill," Ricky said coyly.

"Take it a step further. Agree to the therapy."

"Okay, if that will make you happy, then I will do it. Are you satisfied?"

"Yes Ricky, I'm satisfied." Bianca smiled knowing in her heart they would never participate in a therapy session together. Not in this lifetime. It made her sad, but she wanted to enjoy the moment.

"If we don't get around to seeking help, I hope you will realize your faults and understand that trust holds a high percentage of a successful relationship," said Bianca.

"I know. Now shhh, I want us to enjoy each other. He kissed her on the top of her forehead. He eased her up so he could gulp the rest of his beer. He then positioned Bianca's head back onto him.

"We haven't done this in a while."

"It feels great. Thanks for taking me back B."

They were both soon asleep in each other's arms listening to the contagious soulful sounds of five-time Grammy award winner, Laddy.

CHAPTER 12
BACK TOGETHER AGAIN
BIANCA

Ricky and Bianca woke up Saturday morning in their clothes, still in each other's arms.

"So much for me going back to work yesterday."

"Were you supposed to go back?" Asked Bianca.

"I had planned on getting back to the office by six-thirty."

"Really, what happened?" Bianca sarcastically asked.

"You got me drunk!" They both laughed.

"You're the one who wanted to drink a six pack of beer!" They laughed again.

"Honey, are you hungry?"

"Yeah, let's order food," said Bianca.

"What do you feel like eating?"

"How about sushi and salads from Skippies on Sunset?"

"Baby, I'm from Brooklyn, I need some meat!" Ricky said, laughing.

"Okay, where do you want to order from?" Bianca asked with a smile.

"How about the Italian restaurant we love?"

"Sounds good to me," said Bianca.

Bianca buzzed one of her servants to place the order and have it delivered. He buzzed back to say it would take about an hour.

"We have time to take a shower. By the time we get out, the food should be here. Then we can get in the Jacuzzi," Ricky said with a smile as he entered the shower.

"Come on honey, get in before the water turns cold," Ricky said inviting Bianca into the shower.

"I'm coming. Stop rushing me sweetie."

They sounded like children preparing to go outside. Bianca stepped into the shower.

"Damn you're fine. I mean, I already knew that but, shit! Turn around. Let me wash your back." Ricky stood towering over Bianca's slender body. He washed her back, slid his hands onto her shoulders and began giving her a massage. He maneuvered his hands down to her size 32 *implanted* C cup breasts.

"That feels good." Ricky smiled.

"Of course it does!" said Bianca.

"You are so arrogant."

Ricky worked his hands down her stomach and positioned them onto her private part. Bianca moaned. "Don't start anything you can't finish," Bianca said in a sexy voice. "We're supposed to be taking a quick shower and waiting for the delivery boy."

"Don't worry about the delivery boy. I'm the delivery boy," he whispered in her ear in a sultry voice. Ricky turned Bianca around and seductively kissed her. He gently placed Bianca against the shower wall. He kneeled down to his knees, slowly opened her legs and the rest was all heavy breathing and moans.

"Oh Ricky, this is good. I love you so much."

"Ditto, baby!"

"Ditto," they both repeated and giggled for a second and continued on with the amazing lovemaking. After what seemed to be an eternity, Ricky looked up at Bianca, then stood up to show her how much he loved her. Her facial expression reflected full ecstasy.

"I love you so much, Bianca. I'm so sorry for hurting you."

"You say that now because the sex is good," she said as she kissed him and softly guided her tongue into his mouth.

Ricky pulled her left leg over his, as he entered her and the moans intensified to a mutual exciting climatic point. She needed this. Bianca hadn't had sex in weeks and didn't realize how much her body needed it. It was like the effects of a drug, with her body actually going through a withdrawal.

Bianca grabbed Ricky's butt and palmed it like a ball player palms a basketball. Their hot steamy breath began to fog up the 24-karat gold sliding doors as their bodies intertwined and the water dripped down the middle of his back and between her breasts. The servant called on the intercom to say the food had been delivered, and he was bringing it up.

"Shoot Ricky, the food will be here in 10 minutes," Bianca whispered in a choppy voice while steadily breathing heavily.

"Okay."

They continued to pump as if their lives depended on it. The servant rang the doorbell to Bianca's room. Upon reaching their plateau, Ricky and Bianca yelled out each other's names to confirm a *job* well done.

"Ricky, the doorbell."

"I know, baby. I know." He was delirious and out of breath.

"Damn, that was an hour?"

"I guess so," Bianca was trying to catch her breath as well.

The servant rang one more time. Ricky quickly rinsed himself off, grabbed a towel and got out of the shower. "I'm coming. Calm down," he yelled.

Bianca stayed in the shower leaning against the wall, trying to forget the pain he had caused her in the past, while focusing on the double whammy he had stowed upon her in the present.

Ricky put on a pair of shorts, ran downstairs, and answered the door just as the servant turned to walk away, after leaving the food on a tray. He turned around when he heard the door opening. Ricky thanked him and told him he was sorry for taking so long.

Bianca dressed and walked downstairs in her burnt orange Jean Yu bikini, then went into her private kitchen to get a bottle of wine and Ricky a beer to bring into the Jacuzzi area. She and Ricky got into the warm bubbly water, ate, sipped wine, drank beer, and became oblivious to the world outside.

"My parents are coming in about two weeks."

"I have to fly out to New York to take Negative to an interview at MTV. I also want to see David this time."

"How long are you going to be there?" Bianca asked in between bites.

"Maybe a week or more. I'm going to try and see Adar this time. We're supposed to go out for drinks. I spoke to Armani earlier."

"Tell him I said hello and that he could call me sometimes to say hello. I feel like you are his sibling instead of me." Bianca said laughing.

"I think he secretly wants to be in the music industry!" Ricky joked.

"In what capacity? He never expressed this to me," Bianca said, becoming curious.

"Does he have to tell you everything? He also had some personal things he wanted to consult with me about," said Ricky.

"What personal things? You better tell me."

"Or what?" Ricky stuck his whole tongue in Bianca's mouth and laughed.

"Nothing." She quickly jerked her head away and laughed, wiping her mouth with the back of her hand. "Yuk, you are so nasty."

"You like it."

Bianca ignored his comment. "Just tell me. That's all. When it comes to my younger brothers and sisters, I need to know everything."

"Why would you want to know everything? Don't you think that's having too much information?"

"No, I have lived with them all of my life. The only one that would have too much going on would be Britney. She has what one would call skeletons in her closet! She is the one in the family with baggage."

Ricky picked up his beer and gulped it down swiftly, looking somewhat uncomfortable. "Delaney and I know most of each other's secrets but I'm sure she has some real hidden ones that no one knows. Everyone does."

"You think so? What about you? Do you have skeletons?"

"I was going to say, everyone, except me!"

"Watch yourself! Anyway, Britney is so shady I'm not so sure I want to know," Bianca chuckled as she took a sip of wine.

"Maybe I'll try and come back a day or two early so I can see your mom and dad. I have a lot of things to do in New York so I'm not sure."

"If you can't, it's okay."

"What do you have planned for them?"

"I have a few engagements and lots of meetings to go to. They want to attend the SAG Awards and a few other events."

"I forgot about the SAG Awards. Damn, I'm going to miss that too."

"I think my dad is going to play golf and go fishing with my neighbor."

"Which neighbor?"

"Mr. Randolph, the one down the street with the lovely wife," said Bianca.

"That's nice."

"My mom and I will probably shop like we always do. I also have a few day trips and some meetings, but that's it."

"Well, keep one day free."

"Why?"

"Just do it. You are always asking questions." He smiled then blew Bianca a sexual kiss. The telephone rang.

CHAPTER 13
BIG SIS
BIANCA

Bianca picked up the phone. "Hello."

"Big sis, is that you? What's up? How are ya? You busy?" Asked Britney.

"No, I'm just chilling in the Jacuzzi, having a glass of wine and talking to Ricky." Bianca occasionally glanced at herself in the mirrors surrounding the 450-square-foot, all-white room.

"I'm fine. I thought you and Ricky broke up? Didn't you say a woman should never stay in an emotionally abusive relationship because it only gets worse?"

Bianca didn't respond. She recalled herself having to call home on several occasions regarding her relationship with Ricky. They had broken up many times due to his womanizing acts. But after she found out she was sick, she felt she had to make it work. She strongly believed no one else would love her. She knew she was a beautiful woman on the outside but would be considered tarnished on the inside because of the disease. If she didn't have AIDS she would never put up with this type of treatment.

"Anyway, that is none of your business," said Bianca, sounding appalled that Britney would throw it up in her face. She immediately tried to control her anger. She had just had a great morning. "What are you doing?"

"I'm lying across my bed. I just came from getting a manicure and pedicure." Britney paused. "Well, I called to ask you if I could move to Los Angeles with you for a couple of months."

Bianca really didn't want Britney staying with her. She was too damn spoiled and selfish. Bianca was at a lost for words.

"Bianca, are you there?"

"I'm here." She had gone into a zone before speaking. "Well, what's wrong? Are Mom and Dad getting on your nerves?" She took a gulp of her wine and paused.

"When are they not? That's not even it. I need to be where the action is. I need to show the world just how beautiful and talented I really am!" She laughed. "I just got off the phone with cousin Shana. She's now working for the producer on the Opal Show in Chicago. She suggested I move out of Massachusetts and stay with either her or you. Of course I chose you because you live in L.A. and you *are* my big sis! Plus when Ricky came out here last year for the music convention, he introduced me to a lot of executives, mainly from Los Angeles. They promised to help me. Did he tell you?"

"Yeah, he told me about the music executives that were going to help you." Bianca looked at Ricky and winked. She had tried helping Britney in the past, but for some reason Britney thought she could be a diva without having to put in the time and effort. She started talking to people as if she had been in the industry as long as Diana Ross. Her tone and personality were horrible.

CHAPTER 14
RICKY
QUICK FLASHBACK

As Ricky listened to the conversation between Bianca and Britney he felt his blood pressure rise as if he were 400 pounds, and walking up three flights of outside stairs on the hottest day ever. In his opinion, women talked too much. A flash of he and Britney getting blasted at the convention last year, going up to his hotel suite, and screwing for what seemed like hours, entered his mind. The thought of Bianca's little sister telling him how attractive and sexy he was, now made him feel embarrassed, extremely bad and humiliated that he had taken her bait. She told him she loved a man with light eyes and curly hair.

With him being drunk coupled with her young shapely body, proved too much for him to resist. Afterwards, he realized he had fallen into a bad situation. He had severe regrets, particularly because he hadn't used a condom. He tried to block it out of his mind as best he could, but situations like this crazy phone call from Britney, were always creeping up. He couldn't believe Britney mentioned that music executive crap. Bianca told her Ricky was with her. She knew exactly what she was doing. Britney had the mindset of a guy. Sure there were executives interested in her but only for one thing. Plus they knew she was Bianca's sassy little sister.

Ricky's nerves were shot. He called for a servant to bring him a glass of scotch on the rocks. He drank it fast, then called again for the entire bottle.

CHAPTER 15
BACK TO BRITNEY'S CALL
BIANCA

Britney was so busy running her mouth she didn't realize Bianca had asked her when she wanted to move to California.

"Hello, are you there?"

Bianca looked at Ricky with a disappointed look on her face. "Slow down on the alcohol. Wait for me!" She said to Ricky. "Britney, are you there? When do you want to come here?" She asked again.

"Oh, sorry. Yeah, I'm here. I want to come there in about two months. Is that cool?"

Bianca could hear her brushing her long reddish brown weaved hair.

"In a few months? Darn, you're not playing." Bianca felt bad for sounding annoyed.

"I want to come out there in time to enjoy the summer."

"How about four months? Bianca completely ignored Britney's time frame. "I need time to get myself together. I need to figure out which room I'm going to put you in." Bianca was searching for an out. "In between that time, don't forget about me being on tour."

"What? It's not like I'm a stranger. I can stay in any room when I get there."

"I'm not sure which part of the house I want to put you in." She knew her answers sounded crazy.

Bianca's twelve-bedroom house was featured in magazines and on the hit television show, *Celebrity Estates.* In the center of the house she had a beautiful 100-pound white crystal chandelier, overlooking a large crystal Lion fountain with mineral water shooting from his mouth. This area divided the east and west wing. A full- fledged dinner party could have taken place in her house and she would not have to be involved.

She was searching for any excuse to make Britney change her mind.

"Please sis. It doesn't matter. Pick a room. I don't care if it's the garage! The maid doesn't have to clean my part of the house. I'll clean it," Britney pleaded.

Ricky whispered to Bianca to tell Britney six months.

"Okay, how about six months? This way it will give me some time to clear my head. You know I'm not use to living with anyone."

"That derelict Ricky spends enough time over there cursing you out – he might as well live there."

"Who are you talking to?" Bianca said, sounding irate. She rose up out of the Jacuzzi to sit on the side.

"I apologize. I was out of line."

"You had better watch your words. Who the heck do you think you're talking to? Do you want me to go through the phone and knock you out?"

"I'm really sorry. You're right. I should not have said that. I didn't mean it. Bianca, please let me come."

"Okay, you can come. I will let you know when," Bianca said still mad but trying to calm down.

Britney sounded a little pissed because she didn't get her way. Bianca didn't care at all. She felt she was lucky to be coming to Los Angeles, period.

"Also Bianca, can you pay for my plane ticket?" Britney sounded really nervous. "Only because when I tell Mom and Dad, they will probably be less likely to give me the money because they don't want me to leave." Britney quickly added.

Bianca knew her mom was getting sick of Britney being there because she hadn't done anything with her life since graduation. Bianca's mom was constantly giving her money, which meant it was crippling her sister.

"I have the phone away from my ear just in case you say no." She sounded like her ear was further away from the phone.

Bianca was pissed all over again.

"You all think I'm a money tree. Just because I'm the oldest and wealthiest doesn't mean you are my child and I have to pay for everything. I just paid for you to get your hair done in New York. You never called to say thank you. I'm paying for Adar and Armani's education, which I don't mind because they

are doing something productive with their lives. You're not."
She was pissed to the highest of *pisstivity.*

"Bianca, don't be like that. No one asks you for money."

Bianca's comments were a slip of the tongue. She usually didn't tell her other siblings who were getting money. She was still aggravated from Britney's previous attacks.

"Bianca, you offered to pay the seven thousand dollars for me to get my hair done. I can't believe you're throwing it in my face. Bianca, you are the one that chose the expensive salon on 34th Street and Madison Avenue. You know if I had the money, I would do it for you."

"But you don't have it," Bianca snapped. "Out of all of us, you're the only one not doing anything productive with your life."

"I will, once I get there, and start meeting more people, and trying to get some things going. You don't have to talk like that because you have money, Bianca. You didn't always have money. Forget it; you don't have to pay for my ticket," Britney snapped. "I'm not going to kiss your behind. If you didn't want me to come, all you had to do was say it," she yelled. Britney turned on her CD player. One of their favorite songs on Bianca's first album started to play. Britney immediately hit the stop button.

"You have a lot of nerve, Britney. You're very selfish."

"And you're rude," said Britney. "Witch," she mumbled. Click. Britney slammed down the phone.

Bianca sat on the side of the Jacuzzi with the phone in her right hand listening to the dial tone while Ricky sat next to her looking at her pathetic expression.

"What happened?" asked Ricky.

"Britney hung up on me."

"That is a perfect reason why you should tell her she can not come to Los Angeles. You all spoil her too much."

"You're right but she is my sister and I always said when I became rich my family would not want for anything."

"Suit yourself," said Ricky.

"I should call her back and tell her off." Bianca hit the speed dial. The phone rang a few times.

"Be cool," said Ricky.

"I'll try," said Bianca.

"Hello." Britney answered sounding aggravated.

"It's me. Do not ever hang up the fricken phone on me again. Do you understand, young lady? When someone has something you need, you should try being a lot nicer." There was silence. Britney listened. "Do you hear me speaking to you?"

"I hear you."

"Then answer me," said Bianca.

"I said, I heard you," she snapped.

"Listen, I'm not asking you to kiss anyone's butt." Bianca tried to ease up a little. "You need to change your tone and also your choice of words when speaking to people, especially if they have something that you want. Your attitude is the reason why you're not successful. Your behavior is the reason why no one will take a chance on your career. I will send you the plane ticket, but you check and get the most inexpensive deal. I'm telling you now – don't come out here causing any problems or you will be right back on a plane the very next day." Bianca could feel Britney's energy change drastically.

"I'm not going to cause you any problems, I promise. I'll call the airlines and call you back in a few days."

"I'll be there for Bryce's birthday so let me know then. I need a break from you."

"I thought you weren't going to be able to make the party?"

"I rearranged my schedule and it looks like I can fit it in." Bianca tried to calm down but Britney had gotten under her skin.

"Good. I'll see you soon. Thanks, I'm so happy. I'm going downstairs to tell Mom and Dad. I'm sorry for my behavior," Britney said abruptly. "I'll speak to you later. Love ya. Bye."

"Love you too, brat. Bye."

As the sisters were hanging up, Britney pressed the play button on the CD player again. Bianca's CD, *LOVING HIM UNCONDITIONALLY*, played on Track #5. It was from

Bianca's platinum album.   She told Ricky that her sister was officially moving to Los Angeles.

CHAPTER 16
BETRAYAL – THE MOVIE
BIANCA

    Bianca's alarm went off at 2:00 am. She wanted to hit the snooze button but had to be dressed and ready to go to the set for a call time of four am. She looked over at Ricky as he slept peacefully. She leaned over and gently kissed him on his back.

    It was great that she could shower, throw on a pair of sweats and go without makeup. It was even greater that the bulk of the filming would be done in Los Angeles. As they approached the movie studio lot, Dutch, Bianca's handsome driver handed the security guard his ID along with her movie ID and announced her arrival.

    "Good morning sir, I have Miss Bianca Baxter arriving on set."
The guard came out of his post, checked the car and trunk before going back inside to check his computer. Within minutes he handed Dutch a printout and told him to follow the blue production signs.

    "Have a nice day," said Dutch.

    "You do the same sir," said the lot security guard.
To the right was a huge nearly empty parking lot. There was a white glass building to the left and a small American-style café in front of them. As they turned left and approached the set it looked like New York City. There were lots of fake buildings with Bodegas attached every few blocks. The set designer did an amazing job. They had a little jazz café to really add some New York flavor.

    Bianca was happy to be a part of the cast because it included last year's Academy Award winner and Best Actor for *Gravitation Towards The Mind*, Brett Livingston, as well as Best Supporting Actress, Julia Redbank, in which it also won for Best Picture. Brett was a professional and very kind while Miss Diva, Julia was a piece of work. There was a problem in the beginning because Julia wanted to hire her own hairstylist and wanted the studio to pay the stylist five thousand dollars per day. Finally, the studio agreed. Julia then complained of not having a big enough dressing room or the right type of furniture. Bianca was tempted tell her to get a grip but opted to mind her own business. The studio wound up getting her another dressing room and allowing her to order her own furniture just to shut her up. Bianca had heard the producer say if Julia complained of anything else he would personally kick her you know what! That is what her agent told her.

The first scene was with Allison (played by Julia) and Craig (played by Brett) arguing in their two-story brownstone because she found a hotel receipt and the stay was not with her! She had borrowed his car to go to the grocery store because her car was being serviced for a few hours. As she opened the back door, a piece of paper fell out. She knew she and Brett had not been to the Four Seasons. The date for the hotel and parking said in and out on the same day. Julia had a really bad feeling. Brett was an electrician, so there was no reason for him to be at the Four Seasons, she thought to herself. When she brought the groceries home she inquired about the receipt. Brett looked busted at first, then started an argument about why she had been badgering him about petty things lately. He seemed overly defensive. They began shouting and Brett decided to leave to cool off. Julia, in a frenzy, called Misty (played by Bianca) and asked if she could come over to their place. Brett called Bianca ten minutes after he had gotten off of the phone with Julia.

"She knows about the hotel," Brett told Bianca.

"I know, she told me. We have to be more careful!" He suggested they cool out for a few days until things calmed down at home. Bianca told him he couldn't, but still, he wanted to come over to her house for a few hours to clear his mind! Bianca said she was on her way over to their place to see Julia. She told him she would contact him as soon as she could. She was hopeful that it would be later on that evening.

Bianca's character Misty was the sneaky and deviously jealous best friend who Julia confided in. Playing this character was fun for her because it was the opposite of her personality. It was also somewhat tense because the character was so ruthless. Upon Bianca's arrival at Julia and Brett's place, they decided to sit outside on the steps of Julia's brownstone. She had calmed down from the short breath of tears on the phone. She kept saying she couldn't believe Brett was acting this way. She couldn't believe he was cheating. Her eyes were puffy and she started to cry again.

Bianca's sly character consoled her and suggested that she might have to end the relationship. The camera zoomed in on a close-up of Bianca's mischievous facial expression. As Julia cried, she confessed she and Brett had had their problems in the past but he had never cheated on her. She paused, then spoke again saying, at least to her knowledge he hadn't cheated! Julia felt like he was not to be trusted at that time. Bianca let her know she was there to help her move on, then told her to pack her bags and stay at her place.

"You know I work long hours but I can give you an extra key." Julia turned to Bianca and said she first needed some time to process what was going on.

The Director yelled cut and said it was a wrap. It was almost 10:00 AM. Working on movies was interesting because directors could start wherever they wanted. At times it was like an emotional rollercoaster and Bianca loved rollercoaster's. She was amazed at how similar the film and music industry was. In music you could work on one song for eight to twelve hours. The same was for film. They worked on two scenes the whole day and evening, both of which were fun. They filmed the scene where Julia and Bianca went out a few days later to a bar to take Julia's mind off of Brett. She was staying at Bianca's place. It was the party scene. After a night of drinking, they took a cab back to Bianca's place. Bianca then pretended she was going over to one of her many men's house, instead she went over to Julia and Brett's.

Bianca remembered her first day on a set. She hated it. There were so many people, from production assistants, assistant directors, interns, lighting crew, sound guys, and extras. She felt overwhelmed with all of the stuff going on in her personal life. However, she felt much better now, especially after a few hospital scares for her. She had chronic muscle and joint pain. Another time her body felt radically fatigued. All ailments were caused from her having AIDS. Her doctor requested that she take a break until he could get her poor body under control. Because she opted not to listen, he then told her she absolutely had to work lesser days or eventually her body would shut down permanently. It took the Producer and Director a little longer to complete the film but the Director, without knowing the exact problem, was very understanding, for which Bianca was grateful. She knew she had better pull herself together. She couldn't afford to be ousted to the public. It would end her career. She could see it now:

HEADLINE:
BIANCA BAXTER DIES DUE TO
COMPLICATIONS FROM AIDS

Bianca knew the media could be cruel. One minute you're loved. They bring you up to rapidly tear you town and she knew it could happen all in one day. She had seen it many times.

As Dutch pulled up Bianca said goodbye to everyone and got into the car. She was so tired. She immediately focused on a few items she needed to add to her bag for her trip to Beantown for her nephew's birthday party. It would be nice to see her family. Her parents were set to visit her once she returned form Boston. Then she had to fly out to shoot a few scenes for the movie. Life was hectic.

CHAPTER 17
BRYCE'S BIRTHDAY
BIANCA

Bianca had to put on a happy face for the family. The pressures of maintaining her image, progressing in her career, and keeping her secret, often made her more fatigued.

Bianca and Ricky were the first to board her $13,250,000 private Gulfstream Jet. As she entered her plane, African American Captain Bernard James and two flight attendants, Inya and Onree, greeted her. The ten seater's interior consisted of Sheepskin crew inserts, high gloss walnut laminates, rust brown leather & light colored fabric side panels and deep brown pillow head rests.

"Hi, Miss Baxter, I saw you on late night television the other night. You looked fabulous girl," said Onree as he also complemented her on her Yves St. Laurent shoes.

"Thanks a lot. I appreciate you saying that." She took two sleeping pills as soon as she sat down in her plush seat. She tried to sleep but felt restless. Her body was now immune to the pills. She considered switching brands in the future.

The limousine driver delivered Bianca's bags to Delaney's front door. He made sure her bags were placed inside and that she didn't have any more needs, then left.

"Wow, Delaney and Eric, you went all out." Bianca felt like Pokemon was a part of the family!

"Hello, Miss Star," said Eric.

"Hello, Eric, how are you?" He walked over to give Bianca a big hug and kiss. He quickly took her bags upstairs to the guestroom then came back downstairs to continue the conversation.

"I'm fine," said Eric.

"I know. You can't complain because you have a beautiful wife and son, right?"

The two laughed as they embraced each other again. Bianca started to feel a little at ease. Being around her family gave her a sense of peace, even if it was for a few minutes.

"Aunty Bianca. You did come for my birthday!" Bryce shouted as he ran and jumped into Bianca's arms.

"Hello, my handsome nephew. I told you I would. You are so big."

"Aunty Bianca, come and see my toys."

"Not right now, Bryce. Let Aunty sit down for a minute. She just got off of a long airplane ride," said Delaney.

"She can sit down in my room and play video games."

"Not right now, Bryce. What did your mother say? He is starting to talk back more and more," said Eric.

"Honey, I will play with you later. I promise." Bianca felt bad.

"Oh, all right," said Bryce as he put his head down.

"Come and give me another hug." Bryce ran over to give Bianca another hug. He smelled like he had been dipped in Johnson's Baby Lotion. "You know I love you, right?"

"Yes," said Bryce.

"As soon as I rest a bit I will go upstairs and look at all of your toys. That is a promise."

"Okay." Bryce jumped down and ran upstairs to his room.

Bianca felt bad because she really was tired. Eric was tidying up the house. Delaney and Bianca walked into the kitchen and Bianca sat down at the table as Delaney started preparing the rest of the birthday party favors and last-minute hors d'oeuvres.

"Are you hungry, Bianca?"

"No, I'm cool," said Bianca.

"Mom and Dad should be here any moment."

"I spoke to Dad from the plane. Mom was out shopping," said Bianca.

"What else is new? You would think she made a gazillion dollars!" Said Delaney.

"I bought her some really nice Moshino shoes and a fly Prada bag but I didn't feel like packing them. I figured I would just wait until they came to Los Angeles," said Bianca.

"That's right; Mom and Dad are going to Los Angeles next week?"

"Yes, I'm so excited."

Bryce ran downstairs with a bunch of toys to show Bianca. He ran past Eric and into the kitchen. "Look Aunty." Eric stopped vacuuming and swiftly followed his son.

"Bryce, if you don't take those toys back upstairs..." Both Eric and Delaney said simultaneously. "...Boy, you are going to get a beating on your birthday."

"These are really nice," Bianca said as she whispered to Bryce to take the toys back upstairs before he got into trouble. She promised she would go upstairs shortly so he could show her the rest of his toys.

"Okay," said Bryce.

Bryce left the kitchen and headed for the stairs with his head down. Eric smiled and shook his head.

"See how you have gotten my boy, Delaney! Bryce, you can bring one toy downstairs. We are trying to prepare for your birthday party, man. If you bring all of your toys downstairs, the guests will not have anywhere to sit," said Eric.

"Honey you can play with your toys later," said Delaney. Bryce seemed to feel a little better.

"What are we going to do with that boy?" said Eric. All laughed. The doorbell started to ring repeatedly.

"You already know who that is," said Eric.

"That doggone Britney," Delaney said trying not to swear. "I told her about doing that!" She had a blank expression on her face.

"I'll get it."

"Hello Big Sis. How was your flight?" She hugged and kissed Bianca without waiting for a response. She then picked up all of her shopping bags and squeezed past Bianca and entered into the house.

"Britney, you look so skinny." Bianca looked stunned. "Wow, where did your butt go? I see you have been doing some shopping."

"Yes for my handsome nephew," said Britney. Bianca handed Britney her ticket for Britney's big move to Los Angeles.

"You didn't answer my question. You're as thin as a pole!"

"I have been busy running around taking care of things before my move," said Britney.

"Well you had better make time to eat. You're looking a little too skinny. I don't like you like this," said Bianca.

"I told her she was getting too skinny," said Eric.

"Me too," said Delaney.

"Enough about my weight. Where is my nephew?" Asked Britney.

"I sent him...." Bryce jumped down two steps at a time.

"Aunty Britney. Hi. Are those bags for me?"

"Bryce, please stop jumping and running. You are going to fall. Then you will not be able to open any of your birthday presents."

"Hello, my favorite l'il man. Didn't I see you yesterday? Are you being a good boy? Happy birthday!" Said Britney.

"Can I open one present right now? Pleaseeeeeeeeeeeeeeeeeeeeeeeee," Bryce pleaded.

"Nope. Let's go upstairs so you can put on your birthday outfit that Uncle Armani sent you."

"Okay, Mommy. I'll be back, Aunty Britney and Aunty Bianca."

"Okay, we'll be here." They both smiled at him, the love clearly evident on their faces.

The doorbell rang consistently every five minutes as the guests swiftly arrived.

Mom and Dad came in with loads of gifts. The telephone rang.

"I'll get the phone," shouted Bianca. "Hello, the Livingston residence," she said in her most chipper voice.

"Hey Bianca, its Armani."

"Hey little brother man, how are you?"

"I'm cool. Where is the birthday boy?" Asked Armani.

"He is upstairs with Delaney putting on the outfit you sent him. I'll bring the phone to him." Bianca walked upstairs with the cordless phone trying not to show she was slightly out of breath.

"What time did you get in?" Asked Armani.

"I got in several hours ago. I'm exhausted."

"Did you sleep on the plane at all?"

"I tried but I couldn't." She walked into Bryce's boyish colorful room. "Bryce, someone wants to wish you a happy birthday." Bianca gave the phone to him.

"Hello, it is me the birthday boy, Bryce!" He hesitated. They all laughed.

"He is too much," Delaney commented.

"Hi Uncle Armani," said Bryce.

"He is too funny," said Bianca.

"He is bad. Tell your uncle thank you for your wonderful gift. Tell him it fits."

"Thank you for my gift. My mommy said it fits." Delaney smiled while Bryce talked on the phone. Bryce told Armani he had to go and gave Delaney the phone and ran downstairs, excited to greet his guests.

"Hey Armani, we love you and wish you were here," said Delaney. "I've been up since six a.m. Bryce ran into our room, jumped on our bed, and woke us up. He told us we had to get up right then or we would miss his birthday."

Bianca cracked up.

"He is a mess. Then Adar called about an hour later. I couldn't get up. I worked until really late last night. Eric got up and cooked breakfast. He served Bryce and I breakfast in bed. I wish you could be here as well. Mom and Dad are downstairs. Britney is downstairs too with her wild self. Okay. I will kiss Bryce for you." She paused. "I love you too. Don't work and study too hard. Bye."

There was a lot going on downstairs. The doorbell was still constantly ringing. Bryce's friends and their parents were flowing in.

"Happy Birthday to you.   Happy Birthday to you. Happy Birthday dear Bryce Livingston.   Happy Birthday to you." As everyone sang in unison, Bryce sang along.

"Happy Birthday to me.   Happy Birthday to meeeeee. Happy Birthday to me." He smiled and clapped his little hands.

"Make a wish," Delaney said.

Bryce made a wish. He leaned over and his Pokemon hat slid forward as he blew out his candles. His spit went flying onto his matching Pokemon ice cream cake. "I wish Pokemon would always be my best friend," said Bryce with his commercial-golden smile.

CHAPTER 18
MOM AND DAD'S LOVE
BIANCA

Bianca was back in Los Angeles. It was great for her to spend time with her family. She loved and missed them often. Her parents were going to be in LA for a week. It would take her mind off of her thinking about how busy her schedule was. Bianca had to go out of town for some wrap-ups on another film, and some other business for a few of the days, but she would find them exciting things to do. Her mom would be happy shopping and her Dad would be happy playing golf, bowling or fishing. Bianca had a function to attend but was sure they wouldn't mind. Mia's mother Gina, and Supreme, Bianca's mom were going shopping the day after they arrived. Supreme could shop for days and be content.

Joseph, Bianca's dad, was a very strong, proud man. He had kinky hair, was 5'11 and was the color of Hershey's dark chocolate. The girls got their almond-shaped eyes from his side of the family. Some people described him as being arrogant. He always had to be *the man*, whatever that meant. He pledged Omega Psi Phi at Morehouse College in Atlanta, but didn't graduate because his father died in his sophomore year, and he had to go home to help raise his three younger siblings. He started working at an investment company in the mailroom. His knowledge of the stock market elevated him to Director of Financial Services over a twenty-five-year span. He met Bianca's mom while she was singing in a band at his company's annual Christmas party. Let him tell the story, he swept her off of her feet and was her knight in shining armor! First one to kiss her. First one to do *everything*.

It was not what Bianca's mom had told her! No one else knew the secret but Bianca and she only knew because she was the first born. Her mom had a sexual encounter prior to her dad. It lasted a few months but the hurt lingered for years. Supreme had gotten pregnant by her high school boyfriend the first time they had sex. Through Bianca's grandparents' careful planning she was ordered to have an abortion since she was only sixteen. Bianca's grandfather beat up the boyfriend and his father for creating what he called a bad seed! He was jailed for forty-eight hours. Bianca's grandma had to borrow the money to get him out. It was a big mess. Her mom was banned from dating. She said she didn't even have the desire to date anyway until she met Joseph, Bianca's Dad, years later. Supreme felt it was better to keep Bianca's Dad in the dark. She felt men didn't need to know everything about their women especially if it was before his time. She said she prayed about it and asked God to forgive her and the boyfriend for their sins and to forgive her parents for disobeying God's rules in the Bible.

Every year Joseph planned his retirement party and then canceled the plans because he said he wanted that check to accommodate the lifestyle he thought he had! Fishing, hunting, and card games with his friends.

Supreme, Bianca's mom was a strikingly gorgeous woman who exuded strength in her own way. She was the youngest of seven children. She said she always hated her name because kids teased her about it. They would call her crème, dream, and scheme. They said she thought she was better than everyone. Bianca's grandparents sat Supreme down when she was six and explained how they named her. Before she was born their car was hit by a drunk driver. She started hemorrhaging and the doctors had to deliver Supreme prematurely. She suddenly stopped breathing, then without intervention she again began to breathe on her own. Her parents had been so frightened, the doctors said it was a miracle she survived. They changed her original chosen name from Betty-Jo Ann to Supreme, meaning highest in quality or in power.

Bianca's grandparents treated her special. Supreme was the only petite girl in the family, and her Mom and Dad's favorite. Her siblings laugh about it to this day. Bianca's Mom loved it. She was a pecan complexion with light brown hair which she had recently had cut. It had grown down her back. She felt a woman in her early fifties should have a short haircut because it made her look younger. Supreme got her under-graduate degree from Berkley, College of Music and pledged Delta Sigma Theta Sorority, Incorporated. She was quite pissed when Delaney decided to pledge AKA. Bianca told her mom not to look in her direction because she wasn't into those types of structured organizations. Bianca bragged about pledging ME LOVE ME PHI ME! Supreme's parents discouraged her from pursuing her singing career so she pursued a Masters in Education from Curry College, then received a Ph.D. at Emerson College, all in Massachusetts. For twenty-five years Supreme had been a professor at Emerson College in Boston. She also worked closely with the Director of the Music Department. They put on fabulous musicals every semester. Bianca and her siblings had been to a couple of their shows. The students adored her. Often when Bianca called home Supreme's students were there. They always wanted to speak to her. Bianca was okay with it sometimes but lately she had been in a funk. Her mom loved anything dealing with music which is why she told her husband, if he retired he would be bored because she was not leaving her job any time soon. Bianca didn't believe her dad was interested in retiring either. He would be bored out of his mind!

"So Mom, what time is Gina picking you up?"

"She said she would be here at ten a.m."

"Gosh, I never get to see her. Rocki, can we get some more tea, please?"

Bianca hoped Rocki never quit. As the head housekeeper and cook, she had been wonderful, despite Bianca's bad attitude lately.

"Supreme, would you like more coffee?" asked Rocki.

Bianca and Supreme were sitting at the kitchen table.

"No, I'm fine. I don't want to be wired!" said Supreme.

Joseph entered the kitchen wiping his right eye to clear his vision.

"Good morning, Daddy."

"You woke up just in time for breakfast," said Bianca.

"Good morning, Sunshine," said Supreme. "Are you hungry, sweetheart?"

"Sir, sit down, I will bring your plate," said Rocki.

"What's for breakfast, Rocki? It smells good," said Joseph.

"Eggs, ham, bacon, French toast and grits."

"Wow. I'll take it all." He grabbed a chair.

"Daddy, we thought you were going fishing."

"I changed my mind. I want to relax today."

"Honey, you can come with us," said Supreme.

"Absolutely not," said Joseph.

"Good. I really didn't want you to come anyway! She smiled and blew a kiss at him, as if they were still giddy teens.

"I don't want to hear your mouth!" They all laughed. "Ha ha ha! You're so funny!" said Joseph.

"Daddy, I'll be home by six o'clock," said Bianca.

"Baby girl, I'm fine. I'll probably take a nap, wake up, then go bowling upstairs."

"Don't sleep too late. We have my friend's dinner party this evening," said Bianca.

"I know."

"I'm glad you said that. You know I can get carried away with the whole shopping escapade," said Supreme.

"Yes, we know," Joseph and Bianca said simultaneously.

Bianca handed Supreme an envelope with $200,000 in traveler's checks to go shopping.

At times Bianca didn't feel like going to events. She didn't always feel like smiling at everyone. She felt people were sometimes dirty and she could do without them putting their nasty slimy lips on her. She tried to grin and bare it, but a lot of times it was hard.

Everyone who was anyone filled the place, and as usual, they cased the room to see whom they could go over and schmooze with before taking their seats.

"Hi, how are you?" said Bianca, speaking to Joi, a slender, strong-featured woman in an African print dress. "I haven't seen you in a while. Have you met my parents?"

No," said Joi.

"Mom, Dad, this is Joi. She is an actress on a soap opera and also does commercials."

"I saw you on a commercial earlier," said Joseph. "Hi, how are you, young lady?" Joseph stood up to shake her hand.

"I'm well Sir, thank you."

"Joi, this is my mom, Supreme."

"Hello sweetie," said Bianca's mom. I'm glad to hear you are doing well." She smiled. "You're on my favorite soap opera. I love your character."

"Thanks," said Joi.

"Can everyone take their seats? We're going to start," said a man with a Barry White voice.

"I'm going to go and sit down. I wanted to come over and say hello because I never see you at the spa anymore."

"I've been busy," said Bianca while smiling.

Okay, it was nice seeing you again. Take care."

Joi turned and scurried away on her toes, trying not to break her stiletto heels. The waiter started to place the salads on all of the tables.

"Would you like chicken, salmon or beef?" He went around the table asking. Most people at the table said chicken. Everyone seemed to be on that, *I don't eat beef* kick! To be the rebel, Bianca asked for beef.

"Good evening everyone." The voice came from the stage letting everyone know to stop their chattering. "You all know why we are here. I would first like to say, who said celebrities don't care?" Everyone in the audience clapped. "Who said we're all ruthless? Well, some of you all are rotten to the core!" The crowd laughed and little whispers were heard. "It is sweeps for you actors, album release schedules for you singers, finals for you ball players! Everyone in between, you all are just nuts! Everyone in here knows what I'm talking about. What is the difference between poor crazy people and rich crazy

people? Money! We call rich crazy people unique or eccentric."
Everyone laughed and began to clap their hands in agreement to
pretty much everything he was saying.

"Hi, for those of you who don't know me, you better
hurry up!" The crowd went wild with laughter. "I'm kidding."
He laughed. "I'm not a comedian."

"This guy is funny," my dad whispered to me. Bianca
wiped the tears from her eyes, from laughing so hard.

"My name is Radio Magic." Radio stood at the brown
podium in a fine black pin striped tailored suit. The little hair he
had left was a salt and pepper gray, but his appearance was not
as crisp as usual.

"Yeah," someone yelled out. Everyone stood to their
feet, giving him a standing ovation, and yelling encouraging
words as they clapped.

"Hang in there," a high profile talk show host yelled
from the far-left corner.

"You look great, brother," a well-recognized and
distinguished actor yelled from the back table.

"We love you," a few more people yelled.

"I love you, too. I really do." Radio Magic sincerely
replied.

"You all mean so much to me. I have been in this
industry for thirty years. I have a lot of fond memories."
Everyone sat still trying to grab every word uttered from his
mouth. "As you all know, I have been diagnosed with cancer.
The doctor said I have six months to live." Everyone gasped.
"I'm a black man, so that means six weeks! The doctors will
probably give me something to kill me quicker. Remember the
conspiracy with black men losing their hair at an early age!"
The crowd laughed but the sadness still lingered in the air.
"Back to the subject at hand. I'm in good spirits and have a
strong faith in the black man upstairs."

"Good for you," whispered Supreme. The clapping
started again. "I've lost a tremendous amount of weight because
of the cancer. I'm losing my hair because of the chemotherapy.
I know I don't have to explain this to you, because I'm amongst
my friends and family. How I look doesn't matter."

"That's right, because we got love for you anyway, big man," someone yelled out.

"Thanks. That means a lot to me. Your $50,000 a plate contribution will go to the cancer society to help people who are diagnosed with cancer and don't have our kind of money." The crowd clapped, then there was silence again. "When I'm gone, I want to be remembered for my sense of humor, brilliance, humanity and talent." People were teary-eyed. "Don't cry for me when I'm gone. I want my friends and family to celebrate my life. Although I can't drink with you anymore, I will be getting blasted in heaven along with all of the fallen soldiers of this wonderful industry!"

"I know that is right," a man from the front table said, as he held up a glass that contained an alcoholic beverage.

"I will be with you in spirit. I had a long talk with God. I told him if he wanted me to stop drinking, he could have just made me throw up on my Gators! That would have made me stop for sure. He didn't have to give me cancer!" He laughed and got the crowd to lighten up a bit. Again, the mood was somber but the energy was of faith and hope. "I'm going to step down now," he said after his eloquent speech. "Once again, thank you for coming out to support me and the cancer foundation. From the bottom of my heart I truly appreciate your being here. I love you all and hope you never forget me."

"We will never forget you," a reporter yelled.

"We love you, Radio Magic," an NBA player yelled.

"I love you, too."

The entire audience stood up to clap for what seemed like hours. He tried to hide it, but a tear escaped from the corner of his eye and slid down the side of his face. There was so much love in the room. As Radio Magic stepped down off of the podium, he slipped and stumbled down the four steps. Everyone jumped up. The men at the front table ran to him to provide assistance. Once he stood up, everyone could see he was okay and laughing so hard it made everyone else laugh. He went back up the stairs to the podium, still laughing.

"I'm okay. I want you all to know that that was not a part of my speech! It didn't have anything to do with the cancer situation and lastly, I have never been so embarrassed in my life! I certainly don't want to be remembered for this!" He laughed some more. Now I'm going to try this again. Pray for me." Everyone laughed and the chatter was at a high. He walked slowly down the steps, this time with escorts.

As Bianca looked around the room she knew, for some of them, it may be the last time they would see the man who played R&B music on the radio for 30 years, and blessed them with special appearances, events, interviews and informal private one-on-one conversations. Bianca said a silent prayer and asked God to make his last days filled with peace, joy and happiness.

CHAPTER 19
DECISIONS
RICKY

"Britney is moving out here, man, in a few months. Have you seen or heard from her since you hit it?" Asked Scooter.

"I try to stay away when she is in town but I have seen her a few times."

Scooter and Ricky were sitting at the Ocean Blue Lounge. It was a hangout for some people to feel significant because they worked in the entertainment industry.

"Can I get you guys something to drink?" said the bartender.

"Yeah, I'll have a rum and Coke," said Ricky.

"What are you going to do?" asked Scooter.

"I don't know. Maybe I'll just continue to avoid her." Ricky looked nervous.

"How are you going to do that when she is going to be living with Bianca?"

"I don't know. I'm thinking with our summery weather, she will be out and about. I told Bianca to tell Britney not to come but I didn't want to press the issue."

"I know I asked you before, but, was she good?" said Scooter with a curious look on his face.

Ricky had a smirk on his face. "Man, I was blasted and horny."

"That doesn't answer my question."

"It was just a piece of tail." Ricky didn't look at Scooter. He didn't want to talk about it. He felt bad.

"But was it good? Was it worth it?"

"Okay, since you want to know, I'm ashamed to say it but yes it was good. No, it wasn't worth it." Ricky looked awkward as he finished his drink. "I still feel bad about it. I know I have slept with other girls but they didn't have a connection to Bianca. They've only heard her music or seen her on television." He knew if Bianca had found out about him sleeping with Britney, this time she might kill him. The thought of it made him sick to his stomach. "That being said, Britney was a freaky deek for real!"

Scooter smiled and wanted to know more.

A voice interrupted Scooter and Ricky. "Hey y'all, what's up?" said Larry, a tall, lean fare skinned brother who was the Director of Artist Development at Roundhouse Records and a former Millenium employee. He ordered a drink.

"Hey, man."

"What's up, man?" said Scooter.

"Can I get you gentlemen another drink?" Asked the bartender.

"Yes," Scooter and Ricky said in unison.

"What's up, y'all?" The men nodded their heads as they turned around to say what's up to another friend that walked by. Greg approached the gentlemen.

"Hey Greg, how are you?" asked Scooter.

"Hey," Ricky said nonchalantly, glad the attention was taken off of him. Greg ordered a drink. Scooter seemed to be watching Ricky's facial expressions.

"Why did you look at him like that?" Asked Scooter.

"You know he swings both ways?" Asked Ricky as he maneuvered his stool so Greg couldn't turn around and join in on their conversation.

"I know you told me before. I don't know how you can tell. He looks so masculine. I know that doesn't mean anything. I work with lots of masculine brothers in the studio and I think sometimes they make googily eyes at one another. It's disgusting but as long as they don't disrespect me, I don't care," said Scooter.

"As a matter of fact I can probably look around the room and point out a lot of brothers that I heard swing in this business," said Ricky as he looked around the room. "That's why sometimes I hate Los Angeles. I feel sorry for the women here. Well, sometimes!"

"You feel bad because you can't get to all of them!" They laughed.

"On a more serious note, it really is sad."

"I'm sure it goes on everywhere, Ricky.   I don't understand it.   California is the Mecca of beautiful women." Ricky nodded his head in agreement.   "Still, California is not the only state where a lot of guys are bisexual."

"You mean gay.   There is no such thing as bisexual. They are just gays that are afraid of what society will say and do, so they hide behind a person of the opposite sex."

"Where did you get this information?   Never mind.   I don't want to hear the answer.   I can't take another theory. Okay, tell me this.   Why are you always so consumed with other people's lives?" Asked Scooter.

"I'm not.   It just makes me sick how brothers walk up to you like they are all hardcore..." Scooter interjected.

"They are!   It is just with other men!"   Scooter laughed and slapped himself on his thigh.   "You are disgusting."

Ricky laughed.   "I don't want to talk about this anymore. We both know this industry is full of homosexuals and that's that.   There is nothing we can do about it," said Scooter.

"I know but it pisses me off..."

Scooter interjected again.   "You always have to have the last word.   Get over it.   They are not concerned about you and your lifestyle.   You're giving them too much power."

As the *industry* crowd poured in, Ricky and Scooter looked around to see who was entering the art deco Miami styled scene.   Sexy sleek girls had filled up the white leather lounge chairs and couches. There were white candles on the low Japanese style tables.   On the wall were huge paintings of musicians with abstract figures in the background.   The floor was glass and had visible multi-colored fish swimming in ocean blue water.   The lounge became dimly lit as time moved on.

"Hey Ricky and Scooter, I knew you two lushes would be here," said their boy Tyrone as he slapped them five.   He leaned to the side of them as he waved his hand to motion for the bartender to bring them whatever they were drinking.

"I suppose you are going to say he is gay also?" Scooter whispered to Ricky condescendingly.   "Now you know Tyrone is not gay."

"I know that but I wanted to hear your response," said Scooter.

"You're a psycho. That's my response."

"So what's up, brothers? What are you guys talking about?" Tyrone pulled up a stool.

"You don't want to know," said Scooter giving Ricky a crazy look.

"What's going on with you, Tyrone?" Said Ricky.

"Last week you were ready to strangle your artist backstage," said Scooter.

"Yeah man, that idiot had just finished participating on a panel discussion, then lied and said he would be right back. I told him to hurry up because we had to go to the coliseum for his sound check for the show that evening. He said he was running upstairs to his room. I didn't pay him any attention because I was talking to my counterpart."

"So then what happened?" Asked Ricky and Scooter anxious for him to get to the climax of the story.

"Hey guys," said Felicia and Stacy, two beautiful brown-skinned women whom they knew from the industry, interrupted their heavy conversation.

"Hey ladies," said Ricky.

"Hi Stacy and Felicia. How is it going?" said Scooter wanting to get back to Tyrone's story.

"Good," they both answered at the same time.

"Hello," said Tyrone.

"We're looking for Roslyn. Have you guys seen her?" Asked Stacy, a short healthy looking woman.

"No," said Scooter and Ricky.

"I saw her when I first came in. She was in front of me. She may be on the other side by the pool," said Tyrone.

"Okay, we'll see you guys later," said Stacey.

"Bye, with your fine selves," Ricky said flirtatiously.

Felecia smiled, turned around, said "bye crazy man," and laughed as she walked away. She was a little taller and thinner than Stacy.

"Okay, finish your story, Tyrone."

"Can I have another rum and Coke?" Tyrone asked the bartender.

"Make that two," said Ricky.

"Would you like another drink?" The bartender asked Scooter.

"Yeah, I'll have another beer. Back to your story," said Scooter.

"This dummy decided to have some girl tell me he would meet me at the sound check. The girl said she didn't have any more information."

"Man, these artists are out of control. I know you grilled the girl," said Ricky.

"I did and ended up cursing her out," said Tyrone looking mad. "She was probably some hoochie he had hit the night before. I was so mad. Later, I found out from the police, he had gone out to the side of the hotel, with some guys, to buy some weed and they robbed him."

"What?" Ricky asked in disbelief.

"He walked out with some guys he didn't know?" Asked Scooter.

"Yes, he is so stupid. I asked him why he did it. He said he was from New York and he thought he could tell if someone was going to rob him. Ricky, when you saw me backstage at the concert yelling at him, I had been cursing him out since it happened."

"What did they take?" asked Scooter.

"They took his $10,000 watch. He also had a five-karat cubic zirconia earring in his ear. He said he would have preferred them to rip the fake earring out of his ear than steal his watch. He had been saving his checks for months to get that watch. I told him that was good for him. We weren't able to make the sound check at all. My boss found out about it, and cursed me out. *Stepson* ended up getting bumped to the latter part of the concert. Instead of performing at 10:00 p.m., they stuck him in the 1:00 am slot. We had a six am flight scheduled to get us into L.A. mid-morning, in time for his interview at the radio station. I felt like banging his head against the floor. I was so mad at him. I changed our seats on the flight so he wasn't sitting next to me. I'm sick of dealing with incompetent artists. It's only a few that make it bad for the rest of them, but when it's bad, it is harder. *Stepson* makes me sick because he tries to play it like he has all of these women, and he's from the hood. That punk is from Brooklyn, but from the Heights. He went to Brooklyn Friends, which is one of the most expensive private schools in New York."

"I know about Brooklyn Friends," said Ricky.

"I can go on and on about these hip hoppers, still for every bad one there is one great one."

"True," said Scooter. Ricky and Scooter nodded in agreement.

"Gentlemen, I have to go." Tyrone put his empty glass down on the bar and stood up.

"I'll see you later," said Ricky.

"All right Tyrone. Take care," said Scooter. They slapped each other five and Tyrone disappeared into the crowd.

"I just left the studio dealing with some ghetto-ites. They were suppose to finish a track by a certain time, and messed around and let their time at the studio run out. Now I have to rearrange my schedule because they decided they wanted to be lackadaisical. It's coming out of their budget. I told them to save their receipts whenever they go on retail visits or dinner with producers, managers, head of promotions and or anyone from marketing. They never listen. I tell them to stop bringing all of their friends from around the way to retail visits, performances or dinners. When they get hit with the huge bill, they panic. Then after their album is released and, they have a negative balance, they want to connect chairs to faces and break limbs. I let them know early on, if they step to me it's going be a circus, the adult black version! I'll stop talking about the situation because I am getting mad." Ricky's forehead was wrinkled from frowning. "Sometimes I can't believe these guys."

"I can," said Scooter.

"Hey Ricky." Mia walked over and gave him a hug.

"Hi Mia, how are you?"

"Hi Scooter." She hugged him.

"Hey lady. Long time no see. How are you?"

"I'm great. This is my friend Gloria from school. Gloria, this is Ricky, Bianca's boyfriend and his cousin Scooter."

Gloria said hello and shook their hands. "What are you doing out at an industry bar?" Asked Ricky.

"We just finished taking a really hard exam and decided to come and have a drink. Bianca told me about this place a while ago. I haven't had the chance to try it out," said Mia.

"After that test, we need a couple of drinks," said Gloria.

"What are you ladies drinking? My treat," said Scooter.

"Thanks Scooter but we are going to get a table. We saw you guys and just came over to say hello. Our boyfriends are meeting us."

"So school is going well?" Asked Ricky.

"Yes. It's tough but I'm almost finished so I can't complain."

"That's good. Bianca told me that Britney was thinking about moving out here in a few months."

"Yeah."

"That should be interesting to say the least," said Mia.

"I don't know if Bianca is ready for her," said Ricky.

"Too late now. It looks like the contract is signed! It's a done deal. There may not be any turning back," said Mia.

"Mia, you are definitely in the right profession." Everyone laughed.

"Mia, your table is ready," a voice said over the loudspeaker.

"That's us. We have to go now. Besides Bianca always says it was not ladylike to sit at the bar!" Mia joked.

"I'm not surprised," said Ricky, shaking his head and laughing.

"Take care guys."

"You too, Mia."

"It was nice meeting you gentlemen," said Gloria. They turned and walked away.

"Likewise." They looked at Gloria's butt. "Bye Mia. S-e-e y-o-u l-a-t-e-r Gloria," Scooter said in a flirtatious tone.

"Finish telling me about Britney." Scooter said out of nowhere as he focused his attention back to Ricky.

"Britney?" Ricky sounded puzzled. "I've told you enough."

"No, you haven't."

"And men say that women gossip," said Ricky as he looked at Scooter like he was crazy. "I'm not going to give you that satisfaction because you're too nosey." Basically, we screwed all night. We were in all kinds of positions, 69,72,46,54! I don't even screw Bianca like that. She knew all the right moves. I wondered if Bianca gave her info on me!"

"I wonder if Bianca found out what she would do," said Scooter.

"Kill me, but her sister came on to me. Yo, she had me screaming her name like a woman up in that hotel room." Ricky felt embarrassed while flashing back.

"For Real." Scooter's eyes lit up.

"When I woke up in the hotel the next morning, I had a bad hangover which got worse when I rolled over and saw Britney next to me. I wanted to crawl into a hole."

"I can't believe you did two sisters! What is wrong with you?"

"Stupid. Plain old stupid. I really feel bad about it, but it *was* good!" I can't believe she is considering moving out here. I think Bianca is making a big mistake. Britney is very selfish," said Ricky.

"Look who's talking! You are the king of selfishness," said Scooter.

"Whose side are you on? I'm your damn cousin. I'm not selfish either."

"Ricky, all you care about is making money and meeting the next prettiest woman."

"Screw you." Ricky started to get nervous. "Is that how you really perceive me?"

"Do you think I'm joking?"

"Am I that bad?" Ricky asked.

"Yes," answered Scooter.

"Wow." Ricky asked for a glass of water, took a sip, looked around the room, and with his eyes, said *what's up* to a few more people.

"I have to get out of here. I have a busy day tomorrow," said Scooter.

"Me too. I don't know why I'm acting like it's not going to be a hectic day for me tomorrow. I fly into DC and New York. I think I'll go and visit David when I get to New York. I haven't done that in a while," said Ricky.

"Tell him I said what's up."

"I will."

Scooter got up. Ricky also got up, and staggered a little. They both walked to the door saying goodbye to people along the way.

"All right, man, I'll speak to you later. Have a good night and flight."

"I hope the day runs smoothly. I don't want to have to beat a brother down!"

"You are a nut, Cuz! You better learn to control your temper before it controls you," Scooter laughed.

Ricky thought about Scooter. Sometimes he wanted to punch the shit out of him because he was always trying to lecture someone. Ricky always told him that was probably why he couldn't keep a woman. Ricky had hooked him up with this girl's friend he had been messing with, and she told Ricky her friend said that he talked too much about nothing, and he was small. Ricky laughed and played it off. He knew he couldn't tell Scooter, so he kept it to himself.

"Later, man," said Scooter.

They slapped each other five and got into their cars.

"P-e-a-c-e," said Ricky.

Ricky landed in DC around noon. He wanted to hook up with Armani but their schedules were so hectic, they weren't able to do so. Ricky tried to get him to come out and meet him at a club called *Creamsickles* for happy hour, but that didn't work out either. He would have to catch him on another trip.

CHAPTER 20
BIG APPLE
RICKY

The driver of the car service pulled up to the hotel. "Welcome to the Skyline Hotel," the bellman said as he opened Ricky's door. "Is this your first time here?"

"No, I stay here whenever I'm in New York," said Ricky.

"Good, I'm glad," said the Santa Claus looking man. "Where are you from?"

"Brooklyn," said Ricky.

"Oh yeah?" The bellman looked at him peculiarly.

"Well, I live in Los Angeles now."

"Oh, I was going to ask you if you traveled from Brooklyn to Manhattan to stay here. That's great!" They laughed. "Let me take your bags inside."

Being back home felt good to Ricky. However, smelling the trash on the streets let him know that there was no other place like NYC. Sometimes you had to get away from the California plastic people. The bellman and Ricky walked in separate directions. Ricky walked towards the front desk to check in. The front desk clerk smiled at him flirtatiously and handed him a message as he checked into his usual suite. She was cute so he smiled back. "Thanks." Ricky read the note.

Just wanted to tell you that I love you and I want you to have a stress-free day. Love B.

Ricky smiled. Bianca was the bomb. He was glad they were back together. He looked up and read the clerk's nametag. She was still smiling flirtatiously.

"Nice smile, Maria Sanchez," Ricky said as he turned and walked towards the elevators to go to his Penthouse Suite #1727.

As soon as he got inside and got situated he called Negative to confirm the time he was suppose to meet him downstairs in the lobby.

"Don't be late."

"I'm not going to be late."

"All right Negative, I'll see you at four o'clock. No C.P. time." Ricky took off his shoes and laid down for a moment. AIDS was kicking his butt. He still sometimes cried in the middle of the night when he was alone. He felt cheated that his life would be cut short. People had been asking him what was different about his look. He dismissed their not being able to figure it out because it was really none of their business. He was taking his medications but definitely had his sick moments.

KNOCK-KNOCK-KNOCK. Ricky jumped up. He had to quickly remember where he was. "Okay, Okay, I'm coming. Who is it?"

"It's me, man. Open the door."

Negative knocked again.

"Chill. I'm coming."

He opened the door. "Calm down."

Negative barged into the room. "Thanks man, enjoy your hundred dollars," he said to the bellman as he disappeared away from the door. Ricky sat down on the rose and pale blue colored chair close to the window. He scratched his head. He was still half asleep.

"I've been calling you but got no answer."

"What time is it?" Ricky looked around the room for the clock.

"It's 3:30. Man, I've been calling you from downstairs since 2:45. I called your cell and paged you, too. Finally I went to the bellman and paid him a hundred dollars to let me upstairs."

"Sorry, I was knocked out. I guess I was tired."

Ricky hurried to remove his medications from the nightstand.

"We still have some time. The interview isn't until five o'clock." Ricky said.

"You told me to be here by 4:00. I got here early because I didn't want to hear your mouth."

"I know. I didn't want any discrepancies about the time. That's why I told you to come early."

Negative had an attitude. "I told you I stopped that C.P. bullshit. I wasn't late in Los Angeles last week or DC a few days ago."

"Negative, that is the second time out of fifty."

"At least I made an effort. Give me some credit."

"Next time," said Ricky still yawning.

Negative laughed. "Fuck you."

"Watch your mouth before I bust your ass," said Ricky.

"You and how many family members?"

"I'm going to take a quick shower."

"Hurry up. I don't like being in a hotel room while another man is taking a shower," said Negative. He knew Ricky was paranoid so he figured he would mess with him.

"Boy, please," said Ricky.

"Can you hurry up?"

"Yes, I'll hurry up."

"Did you eat?"

"No and I'm hungry."

"That's why you came over early. Cheap ass," said Ricky.

"It is not. Man, can you go and take your shower?"

"I'm going."

Ricky hurried and got a change of clothes and toiletries then headed to the bathroom to take a shower, and get dressed for Negative's interview.

Steve B: "Look at all the ladies outside, all for you. Has success been hard for you?"

Negative: "Yes and no. Yes, because people look at us on stage and think what we do is easy. It is also hard because on the first album I didn't make any money. On the second album, I didn't understand the music business. I had been offered more money than I had ever seen. In order to stay in the business, changes had to be made. I remember calling the record company to get some money after my first album went double platinum. They told me that I was in the hole by sixty thousand dollars. Second time, I was in the hole twenty thousand dollars. I couldn't figure out what was happening. I called my lawyer, my mama, my boys, everyone."

Ricky shook his head in agreement.

Negative: "My record company sent me a printout of what had happened so my accountant could thoroughly explain it. The bottom line was, I was broke. Umm, then I had to cut off a lot of friends because the jealousy thing kicked in."

Steve B: "So how was it easy for you?"

Negative: "I got so carried away on the hard stuff; I forgot to touch on the good things. I grew up, learned the business and now I'm making money."

There was laughter in the room.

Steve B: "Your first album went double platinum. Your sophomore album went gold. Your third album went platinum. With your junior album being released today, are you nervous?"

Negative: "No, I'm very confident in my work. I have a strong fan base and I have faith."

"Only when it is convenient for him! I'm joking," said Ricky, smiling.

Steve B: "What should we expect on this album that is different from the albums in the past?"

Negative: "This one has me doing a duet with country singer Trish Black. The song is hot the way it's been done. I actually do some singing."

Ricky: "Trust me. It's hot. It's his best album," he said, chiming in.

Steve B: "I didn't know you could sing."

Negative: "I do a little somethin' somethin," said Negative, blushing.

Steve B: "So you're leaving here and going to your instore? Do you want to tell the public where it is? There's only been billboards, flyers, radio interviews and talk of the date and location spread across the city!" Steve B. was hyped.

Negative: "I'm going down the street to HMD after this interview for the biggest instore ever. He yelled. Come over and check me out."

Steve B: "You are headlining a tour with several Hip-Hop artists. Where does the tour begin?"

Negative: "It begins in Chi-town. Can I give a shout out before I leave?"

Steve B: "You have 30 seconds. Do your thing."

Negative: "I want to give a shout out to the head dog of A&R at my label, Ricky Simmons, my boys, Tre, Low Down, Sekou, and Beam Me Up.   To Ma Dukes, to the ladies…" His voice went up a notch. "You know who y'all are.   Stay sweet.   BLOW YOUR MIND in stores NOW.   It is a must have in your possession. Peace. I'm out."

Steve B: "Pick it up. I've heard it. It's the bomb. Good luck, man.   Go out there and sell millions of copies. Make that money."

"Good job, Negative. We got a nice turnout. This one will be another platinum success," Ricky said.

"I hope so, man. In this business you never know."

"I'm going to be out of reach tomorrow for a few hours," said Ricky.

"Please try not to get into trouble. I'll be available after seven. Call me on my cell phone if you need me. Try to get plenty of rest. See you later."

The car door shut and Ricky watched the driver speed off into the heavily lit Times Square, going towards downtown. It was 12:00 a.m. and Ricky was tired.

"Damn, I forgot to check out of the hotel, Ricky mumbled to himself. As he walked a few blocks to the hotel, his mind recaptured the busy night and thought the instore went really well, especially since everything had been so rushed.

It had been a long day for Ricky. He flagged down a yellow cab. *Damn, it's hard for a black man to get a cab in New York, he thought to himself.* He was annoyed because most of the cab drivers were people of color, too.

Ricky's cell phone rang.

"Yeah."

"Is that how you answer your cell phone?" asked the raspy, sultry voice on the other end. "Where are you?" Karen sounded like she was home waiting on the couch with a sexy nightgown on.

"I'm trying to catch a cab. Are you rushing me?" Ricky replied.

"No, I'm making sure you're still coming."

"I told you at the instore I had to make sure Negative was straight and finalize a few things before I could break out. That's why I told you I would meet you at your house because I didn't know what time I would be able to leave."

"Okay, I'll see you when you get here."

"Hey Karen, put on something sexy."

A flash of sorrow came over Ricky's face just as he made the comment.

"You know you don't have to worry about that. See you soon. Be careful," said Karen.

"Okay, I will," said Ricky. Ricky dismissed his guilty thoughts eating at him.

A cab driver with a large turban on his head and olive skin pulled over and Ricky jumped in.

"Hi, I'm going to 136A-1/2 President Street, between 5th and 6th Street in Brooklyn."

"Brooklyn Bridge closed and Manhattan Bridge very congested," the Arabian man said with a heavy accent.

"Just drive," said Ricky wanting the cab driver to drive right away before he had second thoughts.

The cab driver drove towards downtown. The traffic looked thick. "There is construction."

"Would it be better if I took the train?"

"Yes, probably."

"Are you saying this because you don't feel like going to Brooklyn?"

"No, me don't lie to you. There really is construction. You must believe me. If you want to go, I go."

"No. Pull over." Ricky got out of the cab several blocks from where he had been picked up. New York could be kind of weird at night, especially on the A train which ran on the C line and made local stops. This happened to be the first train coming. Ricky got off at West 4th and transferred across the platform and took the F train to 4th Avenue. Ten minutes into the ride, the conductor had to radio in to the police because there was a guy sniffing gasoline on the train. Also on the train was a couple who both resembled Dracula. They were wrestling from seat to seat. They, too, were escorted off the train by *New York's Finest*. A blind beggar got on the train, asking for money, but dodging all of the poles in the middle of each car. *Only in New York would a man pretend he is blind and dodge the poles,* Ricky thought.

Ricky felt bad for going to Karen's house. His feeling insecure often took over his mind. A lot of times it was hard to face Bianca, the woman he truly loved knowing he infected her with AIDS. The pain was often so severe he would drink, heavily, then go home and go to sleep. Bianca could have any guy she wanted on this planet. She was beautiful, smart, likable, and loyal. He wondered why she had picked him in the first place. They were from two different worlds. If only he could turn back his life events. He would definitely cut down on his cheating. He wondered why he flirted and sought after other women. The only conclusion he came up with was fear. He was afraid of being alone in the world. His thoughts were interrupted by some loud college students entering the train. His stop was next.

"Hey lady. Thanks for waiting up for me. Did I take a long time?" asked Ricky.

Karen embraced him with a sweet kiss. "You look good."

"Thanks. I figured you ran into traffic. You look thinner but good," said Karen.

"I have been running around like a crazy man and haven't been working out as much as I would like," Ricky lied.

Ricky walked into Karen's fabulous three-level brownstone.

"I wound up taking the train because the traffic was so horrible."

"Are you hungry?"

"No, I'm tired." Ricky put his bag down and walked into Karen's room and plopped down on the bed. Karen followed.

"Would you mind bringing me my bag? I don't know why I didn't bring it in."

"Of course not, sweetie."

"A person doesn't have to ask what your favorite color is." Ricky looked around the room.

"You say that every time you come to my house."

"I know. Does everything have to be purple? I get dizzy looking at all of this purple. Purple couch. Purple rug. Purple comforter. Purple lingerie. Purple chairs. Purple art." Karen ignored him. "Did you remember to call the car service for in the morning?"

"Yes, it'll be here at 9:00 a.m."

"Good. Thanks."

"Does David know you're coming?"

"No. I hate telling him a date and time because something may come up and I never want to disappoint him. Plus I can show up unannounced. Where is he going to go?" They laughed.

"Don't forget to set your alarm clock."

Karen plopped down on top of Ricky and started to passionately kiss him. It didn't take long for him to respond.

"Hold on, I have to go to the bathroom," said Karen.

"Right now?" Asked Ricky. Bianca's face popped into his head. He felt like shit but rapidly dismissed it.

"Sorry." Karen got up and went to the bathroom as Ricky kept his eyes closed. He rolled over to get comfortable and immediately fell into a comatose sleep.

"Hurry Ricky. I told the driver you were running a little late. He said for you to take your time, but I know them. They'll leave you."

"I'm coming." Ricky tried to grab the breakfast Karen had gotten up extra early to make. He headed for the door with his luggage in one hand and food in the other. He ran back and kissed Karen on the cheek.

"Sorry for last night. I must have been really tired," he whispered.

"It's okay. I'm sure you'll make it up to me some other day. Get some rest. You look a little tired."

Ricky didn't respond as he hurried down the stairwell taking two steps at a time.

"Thanks for waiting, man. I really appreciate it," Ricky said as he got into the Town Car.

"No problem."

"Don't worry, I'll give you a nice tip."

The driver pulled off. "You're going to the State Prison, right?"

"Yes, said Ricky."

"Do you have a relative in there?"

"I'm visiting my childhood friend. He's like a brother to me," Ricky said thinking about when they first met.

"How long is he in for?"

"He's doing some serious time."

"What did he do?"

"First, it was attempted murder." It was still hard for Ricky to come to terms with the fact that now it was murder.

"How long did you say he was in for?"

"I don't know. They keep changing it. It has been about eight years so far."

"That is a long time. Did he kill someone?"

Ricky cringed at the question but gave in to the truth.

"Yeah, but it was warranted." *What a dumb thing to say*, he thought to himself. Sometimes he felt like it was right. It was scary how the mind could snap. For so long he thought he was losing it. It felt like he was coasting through life in a bubble. Not really appreciating the beauty of it, or what was alleged to be the joys of life. When Ricky did begin to sort things out for his own sanity, he got hit with another whammy. *Damn, do men from the ghetto ever get a break?*

"I also thought his sentence was long because his parents couldn't afford a lawyer and he swore at his court-appointed lawyer in the courtroom," said Ricky.

"That would do it. That's too bad."

"I know. It was a messed-up situation."

"So what do you do for work?"

"I work in the music industry. I go out and find artists," said Ricky.

"That sounds cool."

"What kind of artists do you look for?"

"Mostly R&B and Hip-Hop. I have a few pop artists as well."

"I remember picking up these two guys. The smallest one weighed no less than three hundred pounds. They were talking about their jobs as bodyguards for some of the famous artists. Their job was to protect the artists at all costs. They were paid to take a bullet if they had to. The one guy said that he had this rap artist one time that had just finished performing and was coming off the stage. Shots were fired and the rapper didn't know. The bodyguard ran over and knocked him on the floor extremely hard trying to protect him. The rapper took it as the bouncer was attacking him. The rapper started fighting him like never before. He was yelling, 'get the fuck off of me!' The police came and when the rapper realized what had happened, he was extremely embarrassed. He still tried to blame the bodyguard and the guard didn't argue with him because he knew it was for show. He said the rapper had been smoking that stuff."

Ricky cracked up because he fully understood the crazy minds of some of the Hip-Hop artists.

"Man those rappers are crazy. It sounds like they're paranoid too!"

"Some." Ricky felt his eyelids get heavy. "Wake me up when we get there." He didn't wait for a response and was soon into a deep zone of sleep.

"Sir, we're here." The driver looked at Ricky through his rearview mirror. Ricky didn't budge at first. His head was back against the seat and he was slightly snoring. "Hey buddy, we're here." The driver said it a few more times loudly and turned around to look directly at Ricky. Ricky finally opened his eyes a little.

"Okay, I heard you. I'm getting up. Damn, I needed that sleep." Ricky yawned loudly while stretching at the same time. "Thanks man. So you're going to hang out and then come back to pick me up, right?"

"Yes, of course."

"Here is a hundred dollars. Go and get you something to eat."

"I'll see you at 6:00 p.m. Please, don't be late because I'm going to want to get the hell out of this place."

"Sir, I'll be on time. Have a good visit with your friend. Tell him to keep his head up."

"I will." Ricky got out of the Town Car and walked toward the silver gates.

CHAPTER 21
PRISON
RICKY

There were lots of checkpoints at Ossining State Prison aka Sing Sing. It was not a good feeling to have doors lock behind you. However, Ricky was happy that he was able to send David $5,000 a month. David told Ricky they had searches in the morning and random checks of the prisoners as well as the officers. It was still hard for Ricky to talk to David about this. It never got any easier going to this place. To say it was intimidating was an understatement.

"How is your friend?"

"He's doing okay. He said he liked Sing Sing better than Rikers Island. It's a little more civilized. He has been lifting weights and learning a trade. He makes lockers, license plates and is learning how to cook." Ricky laughed at the cooking part. The driver laughed, too.

"He never knew how to cook before. His mother and sisters would cook for him."

"I guess if you have lots of time on your hands, you have to occupy it with something."

"That's true."

"Do you have to work tomorrow? If not, maybe you can get some real rest."

"Unfortunately I have stores to visit and I have to take an artist to a couple of accounts. I never get any rest. That's why I slept so hard on the way down here."

Ricky tried to dose off again but his thinking about David prevented him from doing so. He didn't know how he kept his sanity.

"Thanks for waiting for me." He handed the driver four one hundred dollar bills.

"Wow, thank you sir!" The driver's eyes lit up. "Here's my card in case you need to go back and visit your friend again."

"Thanks, man."

"No, thank you, sir." The driver tried to hand back the money.

"Take it, please. I really appreciate your patience starting from this morning."

"I told you I would take care of you because you really didn't have to wait or drive the eight long hours. Bye, now."

Ricky got out of the car and headed towards the airport terminal. He decided to contact his doctor to let him know he needed another prescription, because he was all out of refills. He suddenly felt sick to his stomach thinking about all of the pills he would have to consume for the rest of his life.

CHAPTER 22
HARD TO SAY GOODBYE
BIANCA

Bianca's parents left after being in Los Angeles for a week. They had a wonderful time. She took them to a lot of the newer restaurants and they again expressed how proud they were of her. *The Garden* was a black owned restaurant they really enjoyed. The ambience was exquisite. The food was equally as fabulous. Bianca hoped they wouldn't lose what she called the elitist soul and become commercial like some of the other restaurants she frequented throughout the country. Her dad loved the food so much he made a reservation for dinner while Bianca was on a day trip, had her driver take him, then dragged her back there when she returned. She didn't mind because she loved looking at the décor of the restaurant as well as eating the great food.

It was sometimes annoying for fans to come up to Bianca while she was at a restaurant. Sometimes she wanted to be left alone and treated like a regular human being. There were a couple of times when her dad had to be forceful with the tongue because people often assumed that celebrities wanted to put their fork down and turn the restaurant into an autograph signing session. The worst is when a parent would send their teenager over to her. Bianca loved children and couldn't imagine turning down a teen or child. Needless to say, she was so sad to see her parents leave.

"American Airlines is now boarding rows twelve and back," said the ticket agent.

"Honey, that's us," said Supreme to Joseph.

"I don't want you all to leave. Can't you stay another week?"

"We would love to stay but we know you have a lot of work to do," said Joseph. Aren't you going out of town?"

"Yes, I'm flying into Miami to do a photo shoot for my upcoming film. I'll be back for a day, then I'm off to New York."

"Good, you can see your brother."

"I know. I'm looking forward to that."

"We had so much fun. I don't get to spend time with you that often, especially since my music and acting take up so much of it."

"We had a wonderful time sweetie and we will be back." Her mom gave her a big tight hug as they rocked back and forth. She let go and kissed Bianca on her forehead and cheek. "I love you, honey. "Tell Ricky we said thanks for everything."

"Okay. I love you too, Mommy."

Joseph smiled and stared at them, a proud expression on his face. "Come here, my little pumpkin." Her dad grabbed her then hugged and kissed her on the cheek.

"Tell him your mother said thanks for everything!"

"Last call to board the plane," said the ticket agent. They looked around and everyone had boarded except for them.

"We better get on board," said Supreme. Bianca walked with them until she couldn't go any further. She gave her parents one more hug and waved goodbye.

"We love you, honey, and remember what I always tell you. If things get too hectic in this fake ass town…"

"Please honey, we're in public," Supreme interjected.

"I just want her to know she can always come home," said Joseph looking innocent.

"Come on," said Supreme.

Bianca smiled while watching her parents have a mini argument as they walked down the corridor to board the plane. They made a slight left and Bianca could no longer see them.

Bianca turned around, walked to the parking garage, double clicked her alarm, and got in her car. She sat there laughing to herself about how open and honest her father was and how her mom sometimes candy-coated things, including his behavior. However, they were still the bomb as parents. Her mom had a different way of expressing herself. She often thought about other people's feelings, even if they hurt hers. However, she would probably hit someone with a baseball bat if they messed with her family! Out of all of her brothers and sisters, Bianca probably took after her mom. Bianca often wished that she had her father's personality when dealing with Ricky.

She started the engine and pressed play on her CD player. She pressed track #10. The soothing sounds of Eric Taylor came on. Because she was a singer, she hardly ever went to concerts, but had seen him several times. Eric opened for one of her shows and they were good friends. His energy on records was incredible. The world just didn't get his vibe right now. It started to drizzle as she got onto the 405 heading towards the 10 freeway. She hated rain. She wished she'd let her driver take them to the airport. She started to sing along with the words.

"You cross my mind all of the time,
I remember the love in your heart.
You told me only a week ago;
You loved me from the start.
Your scent still lingers here,
The stares in your eyes,
Show the soul doesn't lie.
You said you would not leave me.
I want you back,
Please hold me for at least a day,
Do you understand my pain?
I don't know if my heart hurts,
Or if I'm just insane."

Bianca thought about her relationship with Ricky and instantly became sad. Her mom always told them, "love relationships should not be filled with confusion." She whispered as she felt tears roll down her face. She was hoping to wake up one day and the relationship would not be as intense. If it ever got out about her sickness she would be furious and ashamed. She knew one day it might leak especially with Ricky screwing around. That day would surely be the day she'd wished she were dead. Having had her parents there was a great diversion for her to not delve into blood boiling disheartening thoughts about her future. She begged her parents to stay longer. They temporarily kept her mind off of her secret. She also enjoyed their company. She often discussed her relationship about immature Ricky with Mia but not at length. It was too painful.

The sun started to set behind the clouds. Bianca felt like her tears had become a part of her secret life. She had a wonderful singing and acting career. When she opened her mouth it mesmerized everyone. The way she moved her body on stage and off captivated her audience. People stopped and stared wherever she went. Her inner beauty was the perfect match for her outside appearance. Her life should be great, she thought. Mia was the most positive loving friend she had ever had. There was not anything Mia wouldn't do for her. Bianca's family was close, very thoughtful and loving. She believed even Britney with her spoiled self, still loved her big sister. Bianca had an education from one of the top schools in the country. Yet, she continued to go through this sense of not feeling whole. When alone, she sometimes felt a huge disconnect with the universe, which caused her to have emotional breakdown moments, and feel disheveled at times.

Nothing seemed to matter to her, when the feeling of a crazy relationship consumed her and she felt such mental anguish it caused physical pain. Bianca thought about her situation at least once a day. Ricky was suppose to meet her at the airport, but said he had to go to New York at the last minute, again. Bianca felt stupid but took Ricky's word anyway. She tried to give him the benefit of the doubt. She was too drained to argue. She told him she loved him and would see him when he returned. She also called and left a sweet message at the hotel where he *said* he was staying. Although she called him and left a message on his cell phone, he hadn't returned her call yet. Her parents asked where he was. She told them he had to go to New York. Bianca didn't think her dad liked him anymore. She assumed it was probably because she was always calling home and discussing the bad things that happened between them, with the exception of her disease. Ricky had taken them out to dinner a couple of times while they were in Los Angeles. He gave them tickets to see the Temptations. He paid for them to go to Lake Tahoe for the day. He had planned this when he found out they were coming. Bianca was happily surprised.

Bianca thought Ricky's thoughtfulness gave him some *cool* points considering he hardly took her anywhere anymore. He had in the past, but she had been catching him in more lies lately.

Her dad wasn't buying it. He said he could have purchased the tickets himself if Bianca would have told him where to pick them up. Joseph could be a piece of work. Bianca realized she had been thinking for a long time because her exit was coming up next. She put her right blinker on and merged into the right lane to exit off of the freeway at Sunset Boulevard.

Bianca waved to her security guards as she drove onto her property. She clicked her garage door opener, pulled in and got out. She walked up the two steps through the garage. She could hear her cell phone in her purse ringing. As her servant opened her door, she rushed inside while fumbling through her large purse to find her palm phone.

"Hello." Bianca snatched.

"Hey girl, how are you?"

"Hey Mia, what's up? I was thinking about you."

"Did your parents leave?"

"Yes, I just dropped them off at the airport. I wanted some alone time with them with no servants and or boyfriends. I had such a nice time with them. I miss them already." Bianca said putting her belongings down on one of her sixteen mustard yellow colored kitchen chairs.

"I'm glad. Well, are you sitting down?"

"No, should I be?" Bianca asked, feeling nervous.

"Yes," said Mia.

"What's wrong? Are you okay?" Bianca focused intensely on her conversation, and flung her hair out of her face with her orange sunglasses.

"Girl, I'm wonderful.   Are you ready?   I'm getting married!"

Bianca screamed with joy. Her servants and Rocki were used to her loud mouth.   They looked up and smiled but continued their duties as usual. "When did this happen?"

"Last night. I would have called you then but I spent the night repaying Thomas for the size of the ring he bought me!"

"You are so crazy. Congratulations. I'm really happy for you, Mia.   Okay, what size is the ring and when is the wedding?"

"My ring is five karats and the wedding is set for May 10, my grandmother's birthday." They both said it at the same time.

"That is really sweet of you. Why so soon?   Are you pregnant?" Shouted Bianca happily.

"Hell, no.   You know I would have told you that immediately."

"I'm graduating this year and will be taking the bar exam in July, so I won't be getting pregnant any time soon."

"It will be hard taking the bar so soon after your wedding and graduation, but I know you, the one who defeats the inevitable.   I remember in college you took eight classes to graduate and even made the Dean's List.   That was truly a miracle. What is the urgency to get married?" asked Bianca.

"There is no urgency. You know me. I always do things last minute," said Mia.

"But why rush your wedding?"

"We don't feel like planning an elaborate wedding. I'm sure my mom and grandma will debate with me on this. We want it to be really small, therefore we won't have much time to plan."

"It's your choice and you know I will support you in whatever you do."

"Thanks girl," said Mia. "Are you okay, Bianca? You don't sound like the normal you."

"I'm fine," said Bianca.

"Bianca it's me, Mia."

"I don't want to spoil your happiness. I'm beautiful."
As soon as Bianca let the words beautiful roll off of her tongue,
she remembered five minutes prior, she hadn't felt so beautiful.
She made her way onto the living room couch so she could
continue her conversation. "Tell me about your wedding plans."

"I haven't decided anything yet. I needed to speak to
you, my maid of honor first."

"Mia, I'm honored." Bianca expressed pure happiness
for her friend as she got teary eyed.

"What the hell did you expect? Now I know something
must be wrong. You knew you would be the maid of honor at
my wedding. We have been talking about this since college.
Mia, I'm honored? She mimicked Bianca. What is going on,
Bianca? Don't worry about my wedding plans. Talk to me."

"I'm fine." Bianca dismissed Mia's question and
continued on about the wedding. "Let's talk about your plans.
Really there is nothing wrong with me. There was a lot of traffic
on the way home and now I'm tired. You know I never drive
anywhere and if I do and there is traffic it stresses me a little.
That's all. I want to talk about you."

"Alright, when do you want to meet?"

"Probably this week. The earlier the better because the
latter part of this week I fly to Atlanta to work with a producer
on a song. We're taking my plane so you're welcome to come
with me and we can discuss it then."

"No, I'm too swamped. How about Wednesday?" asked
Mia.

"Tuesday morning is better for me. I'll have my driver
pick you up."

"Are you sure you're fine Bianca?"

"Yes girl, I'm fine and ecstatic for you." Bianca smiled
as she sat up.

"Okay, I'll speak to you later. If you need to talk, I'm
here for you."

"I know you are. You always have been. I love you and
am very happy for you. See you on Tuesday."

"I love you, too. See you then." Mia hung up the
phone.

Bianca stood in her living room with her phone in her hand thinking. *Wow, Mia is getting married.* She had heard through other people that two of the girls that were her roommates after college had gotten married. She wondered if it would ever be her.

CHAPTER 23
JETSETTING
BIANCA

Bianca continuously had to cancel meetings with Mia because her schedule was too hectic. Her life was consumed with going to awards shows. She loved going to the Grammys, the Video Music Awards, the Academy Awards, and the British Awards. She enjoyed those times of the year because she knew she would end up with at least 20 dresses from all of the hottest designers. She still remembers the first dress she wore to the Grammys. It was a long black dress with a two-foot train in the back. The front was a V that went down to her belly button with a chain across the breast. It was very classy and had all of the critics snapping pictures and talking. They perceived Bianca was into clothes but purchasing shoes was the huge part of her life.

At the Academy Awards, when Bianca approached the red carpet, a gentleman directed her and Ricky where to check in, and get their credentials. As they walked down the beginning of the red carpet they stopped at the picture stage to take a photo, which was to be picked up at the after party. Cameras were flashing on the left and fans were cheering from the high school football game-type bleachers on the right.

"Over here Bianca," said one photographer.

"Bianca, look this way," said another photographer.

"We love you Miss B," said a fan from the bleachers.

Bianca waved in both directions. "I love you too," she said to a fan.

A well-known entertainment reporter stopped Bianca for an interview. The cameras were still flashing. Bianca was pulled away for three other interviews prior to reaching the end of the carpet walk. She stopped to hug and say hello to old friends in the industry. As Bianca passed by a celebrity woman being interviewed, a reporter immediately cut the interview short to get to Bianca. Ricky smiled as he stood in the background of Bianca's noticeable fame. Right before she entered the famous Kodak Theater she completed one more interview, posed for a shot, blew a kiss to her fans and gracefully entered the building.

Walking the carpet was always fun for Bianca because she looked forward to the strut as well as the attention.

Bianca's professional life was demanding. It was pissing her off that she again was canceling meetings with Mia but Mia consistently reminded her that she asked God for her fame so she shouldn't complain. Still, Bianca felt bad.

"You just better be at my darn wedding standing beside me! Thank God for computers," she would say.

Bianca promised her that she would be there. Mia emailed pictures of dresses and asked for Bianca's opinions. Bianca found time to pick out her dress and help Mia pick out the bridesmaid dresses. The wedding party was small. They used one of Bianca's favorite designers. Veromica and Portia were bridesmaids and Mia's childhood friends. Bianca really liked them and felt they were true friends. No jealousy, apprehensiveness, drama, or anything like that going on. Bianca knew the wedding would turn out beautifully because Mia and her family were upper middle-class people, that is except for her brother Ronnie, who was in prison.

It happened a few years before Mia and Bianca met. Ronnie went to prison in the late 80's for attempted murder and was not getting out until a few years into the 21st Century. Shortly after he and one of his many bitter girlfriends had had a baby.

He and his boys were zooted at a late-night house party in Compton when he said a guy disrespected him so he tried to blast him out of this world. It was not what the police report said. They seemed to think it was a gang initiation shooting. He was a medium built brother with one dimple and the most beautiful smile Bianca had ever seen. Although he tried to be strong, you could see a sense of sadness and regret in his eyes.

Mia said there had been signs of his involvement in a gang but he never admitted it. She was upset about it but said in life you made choices, he chose the wrong path, and had to suffer the consequences. She said he had the same opportunities she had.

This was the reason she decided to become a lawyer to prove that she could overcome being a product of her environment. Compton was rough but not as bad at its reputation. The media hype made it seem a lot worse. It was equivalent to the reports saying Bedford Stuyvesant in Brooklyn, New York or the Cabrini Green projects in Chicago were one of the worst neighborhoods in the country. Ricky is from Brooklyn. He said it was not as bad as the media portrayed it to be. It was the same thing with people hyping up areas that were not all that, such as the Hamptons and Martha's Vineyard. Bianca had seen much more refined areas in other countries and in Los Angeles alone. The Hamptons and Vineyard were nice but not impressive.

Mia visited Ronnie as often as possible. However, the last couple of years had been hectic with school, study groups and practically living at the library. Bianca went with and without her on several occasions. They were exactly opposite from Bianca's brothers. Mia's grandmother and mom went often. Bianca knew it saddened them too, but they knew they had to be strong for Ronnie. They cooked lots of food for the trip and got decked out from head to toe as if they were going to church.

Bianca had called Mia's mom, Anita Baker and her Grandmother, Diahann Caroll since their sophomore year. Her great grandmother had her grandmother at sixteen and the cycle continued down to her mom, then to Ronnie. It skipped Mia because she was determined to do better. Her mom made sure of that. Ronnie had a baby at sixteen but the family hardly got to see her because Shamika, the mother, moved to East Oakland when Shaneema was seven. She was always bugging for reasons they didn't understand. Ronnie had plenty of women when they got together, but she knew that every time she laid down with him. Knowing Mia, her mom and grandmother, Bianca was surprised that he ended up in that situation.

Mia got fed up with Shamika promising to let Shaneema spend time with them then standing them up, she went over there and threatened to beat her up. Shortly after that, Shamika's mom said they moved to Oakland and wouldn't reveal the location.

Straight-up ghetto gurus! Her mom and grandmother were hurt and mad but after a few months they realized Shamika would have done something else drastic anyway.

Bianca looked at the clock and realized she had one hour to get dressed. The car along with Buggy and Peewee, her bodyguards, would be there shortly to take her to the airport.

New York was a cool city to visit. Living there would be a different story. It was so dirty. Bianca didn't understand why people loved the city. It had a stinky smell to her. However, she did like the flava it had to offer and loved the food and view from New York City Lights, a restaurant overlooking all of New York and Jersey City.

Bianca was waiting for Adar and Sandi so she could give them tickets to Madison Square Garden for that night's show. She had some time to kill and figured she would catch a bite with her brother and his girlfriend as she looked at the beautiful view. Buggy and Peewee were both on their cell phones so they had removed themselves from the table. Her mind wandered back to the early years of her career when she performed at the Apollo in Harlem.

That night she was in her dressing room when someone knocked and said she was up next on stage. All of a sudden she got so nervous. She almost threw up while walking down the steep rickety wooden stairs on her way to the stage. Ill feelings were moving through her head like, what if they boo her? She knew they weren't suppose to boo the musical guest, but heck, black people are hard on performers! She thought, what if someone threw a tomato and it splat on the side of her face and the cameraman captured the moment with a close up shot? What if she opened her mouth and nothing came out? What if she tripped over the thick good luck log? As she approached the curtain she knew she had better snap out of her crazy thoughts because this was it. She had one shot to show the world she was not just a pretty face and beautiful body. She was Bianca Baxter, Joseph and Supreme Baxter's eldest child, a talent not to be compared to anyone of her generation, an all nat-ur-al, no preservatives, sprinkled strategically with organically grown brown sugar, and a dash of cinnamon, to add flavor, a true star-rah! She opened her mouth and hit the first note from Whitney Houston's song, *I Will Always Love You*. Ricky thought it would be better for her to sing this song first and then come back with her hit single. A man from the back of the historical small theatre yelled out that he would be happy to share Bianca's love and life! Another guy in the balcony yelled out he would love to take her, for all she was, and ever hoped to be, with her fine self! Bianca smiled and waved and stayed right on track with the rest of the song. She worked the entire stage with her black patent leather thigh high boots and black cat suit. A middle-aged woman in the second row with a dried out curly hairstyle known as a jerry curl, yelled out for her to sing that song. Bianca did what she was told. She got a standing ovation. She thanked the Apollo audience so profusely Ricky was signaling from the right side of the stage for her to get off of the stage! She did one more princess bow and swiftly exited the stage, passing the good luck log and touching it one more time for her next performance. That night she felt as eloquent as the fabulous Diana Ross. She still secretly laughed to herself about that day. She never shared her panic attacks with anyone because the story would not have been as dramatically interesting if she repeated it. It was one of those situations where one would have had not only had to be there but also to have been in her mind to understand the complete story.

"Excuse me Miss, aren't you Bianca Baxter?" Her thoughts were interrupted. Bianca looked up.

"Yes."

"Oh my God I love your music. My favorite song is HONEST MISTAKES. Can I have your autograph?"

"Sure." The mid forty-ish olive skin toned woman handed her a napkin and a pen. Her hands trembled. Bianca signed her name after writing her a message. *Thanks for loving my music. May you be blessed enough to dream big.*

"Thank you so much."

"What is your name?" Asked Bianca.

"My name is Maureen Welch."

"Have a blessed day, Maureen."

"You do the same, Miss Baxter." She walked away smiling.

"You know everyone is going to start coming over here for an autograph," said Peewee pulling his chair back out at the table.

"I know and I'm really not in the mood. Peewee, you have to tell them no autographs and be adamant and not mean."

"I know," said Peewee, whose name did not describe his physique. Buggy walked over to the table and sat down. A medium built man approached them.

"Can I help you?" Asked Buggy.

"Yes, I would like to say what's up to Miss Baxter." He was a short, middle-aged man with a nice, expensive suit, but cheap shoes.

"She's a little busy right now. She's not signing any autographs at this time," said Buggy.

Bianca pretended to be engrossed in a conversation with Peewee and occasionally glanced out of the window. The view was absolutely breathtaking from the 107th floor and was often captured on postcards and sold in gift shops throughout the city.

Buggy got rid of the guy and the several other fans that decided to walk over. Buggy turned to join in their conversation as Bianca got up and walked closer to the window.

"Hi, I'm the manager. My name is Mr. Goldberf and I'm new here. Is everything okay? Great view, huh, Miss Baxter?"

"Yes, I sit at this same table every time I come here. I just wanted to stand here for a moment."

"As I said, I'm new and was told to make sure you were taken care of and didn't need anything."

"I'm fine Mr. Goldberf, you are doing a wonderful job."

"Thank you. Please let me know if you need anything."

"I will. Thank you again."

Mr. Goldberf disappeared into the back of the restaurant.

"Check this out. One guy offered me a hundred dollars just to let me allow him to shake your hand."

"What did you say?" Bianca laughed.

"I told him after you fired me, I would need more than his one hundred dollars!"

Everyone laughed.

"Isn't the skyline breathtaking?" Remarked Bianca.

"It is nice," said Buggy. You come here every time you come to New York and say the same thing. What is the difference this time?"

"Nothing, I'm just being reflective," said Bianca.

Buggy looked up and smiled but quickly concealed his facial expression.

"What are you smiling at?"

"Nothing. I was just thinking about something that happened at home. It's nothing big."

"Well, you sure are smiling like it was big. I will not ask you to share." She laughed and reached up and hit his shoulder. "It seems personal." They laughed.

Adar and Sandi snuck up and tapped Bianca on her shoulder.

"Excuse me Miss, can I speak to you for a moment?"

Bianca turned around and her face lit up. She gave Buggy a fake evil look because she realized why he had been smiling.

"Hello brother." They hugged each other tightly. "Hello Sandi, how are you?" Bianca did the same to her.

"Girl, I'm great," said Sandi.

"It is so good to see both of you."

"It is good to see you too," said Sandi.

"Our table is right there. I just wanted to look at the sights. We can sit down and order."

The food was great. Bianca got her usual chopped salmon salad with a glass of red wine. It was nice sitting with Adar and Sandi talking about school and life in general. The time went by fast.

They got up to catch the elevator to the lobby. It always amazed Bianca how quickly the burgundy plush elevator got to the lobby.

The Black Lexis stretch limousine was waiting to take them to Madison Square Garden. Looking out the window at the cab drivers was always scary to her. Especially the way they made right turns from the left lane. No blinker. No warning. Nothing. Everyone else in the limo looked as if it was the norm. Peewee and Buggy loved the excitement.

CHAPTER 24
CONFERENCE CALL
RICKY

Ricky was exhausted. Bianca kept telling Ricky that he needed to take vitamins. He was taking his prescribed medications and even that was difficult for him to remember. He knew he had to slow down. Between the conference calls twice a week, running from city to city via car, train and plane was killing him. He was glad he had missed the call last Monday.

"Good morning, Roberta.

"Good morning, Ricky. Your conference call is getting ready to start. Bianca just called you again. She said to call her on her cell phone."

"Are there any more messages?"

"Yes." She reached for the messages in his inbox.

"Nicole, Scooter, Beverly and your doctor's office called to confirm your appointment for tomorrow morning."

"Thanks." He did forget. He took the messages and walked to his office. He shut the door and placed everything down on his Oakwood desk. He had a couple of minutes before his conference call started. He called Beverly back.

"Good morning, Beverly." She was a short, striking woman with a pointy nose and a long reddish-brown, curly weave. When he first met her he thought she resembled Shante' Moore. He remembered imagining the positions he wanted to have her in. He fulfilled half of them! He had to come to the realization that the other positions may not come to pass. One time they were having intense sex and the condom broke. It was so good, they kept going. They regretted it later. He usually didn't slide on using a condom because he didn't want to infect anyone. He thought if she was pregnant, he would give her the money for the abortion and if he were in town, he would even go with her to the clinic. He made a promise to himself not to let any more slip-ups happen because he certainly didn't want to pass on his sickness again.

"Good morning, beautiful black man. How are you?"

"I'm a little tired but I'll live. What's going on, pretty lady?" asked Ricky.

"I wanted to know if you were free for dinner tomorrow night."

"I'm sorry, I'm not. I have to go out of town. Can I take a rain check?"

"Sure, when is a good time?" asked Beverly.

"In a couple of weeks because I'll be in and out of town," said Ricky.

"I thought you were going to make time for me?" said Beverly in an annoying whiny voice.

"Sweetie, I have made time for you but I also told you I was a busy man. I'm sorry. You know I travel a lot. Maybe when I get back we can spend a couple of days together." Ricky knew when that statement rolled off of his tongue that it wasn't going to happen. His other line rang. He wanted to call Bianca back before his conference call because the call would take hours.

"Bev, that is my conference call, I have to go," he said interrupting her boring speech about how she wanted to see him.

"Call me back." "Okay. Take care. I mean okay. I will call you back. Bye."
He wasn't going to call her back. At least it wouldn't be today. He pressed the blinking button.

"Hello, this is Ricky."

"Ricky, this is your conference call," said Roberta.

"Okay," thanks.

"Hi Ricky, please state your name and title," said the operator with her hollow voice. The industry was so pretentious.

"Ricky Simmons, Senior Vice President of A&R," he said almost forgetting about his new promotion.

After what seemed like years, the boring call was finally over. Ricky wanted to call Bianca back before he forgot. She had left him several messages. She should be on her way back to Los Angeles. His private line rang as he dialed her number.

"Hello, this is Ricky."

"Hey, honey."

"Hi, I was just calling you."

"I called you this morning," said Bianca.

"I know. I got in a few minutes before my conference call."

"I got stuck in an interview and won't be able to get there until morning."

"Did you call Mia?"

"No, I don't want to burden her again with my cancellation. She said if I couldn't make it, it was okay."

"I saw her," said Ricky.

"Really, where did you see her?" Bianca asked.

"I forgot to tell you. I saw her at the bar with her girlfriend from school."

"Really, when?"

"It was a few days before I left to go away. They were meeting their boyfriends."

"That's nice. She needs to get out. I have to go. I wanted to tell you I was going to be coming in on a Red Eye."

"You sound stressed."

"I'm...."

"Is there anything I can do?" asked Ricky as he mistakenly interrupted her.

"You can pick me up at the Airport Hangar in Santa Monica," said Bianca. "We're coming in on my plane."

"Consider it done."

"I have to do another interview at the television station and a photo shoot."

"Tell everyone I said hello. Call me at home later. I'm going to be there getting some rest," said Ricky.

"I will," said Bianca.

"If I don't answer, leave your information on my machine. You know I sleep hard when I'm tired." At that moment Ricky knew she wasn't going to believe him, so he told her to keep trying for a few times and he would possibly wake up. He had been fatigued more than usual lately. If only he had someone to discuss his sickness. The only one that knew was his mom and Bianca. He never felt up to having any lengthy discussions with her. He could only think about how he was going to hit his bed so hard it might break!

"I have to go, they're calling me. I love you," said Bianca.

"I love you too. See you at the airport."

They hung up.

CHAPTER 25
BACK IN TOWN
BIANCA

"Hi, sweetie. Thanks for picking me up." They kissed long and hard. "Sometimes I want to feel normal and have your beautiful face pick me up."

"Did you call Mia?"

"Yes. She was very understanding. The only thing she said was, *your butt better be at my wedding standing by my side.* I'm going to go over there tonight and we are going to go over the wedding plans."

"Aren't you leaving in the morning?" asked Ricky, looking slightly puzzled.

"Yes."

"Why didn't you just fly straight to Denver from New York?"

"I didn't want to sleep on the plane. I wanted to sleep in my own bed. Don't you want to see me?" Bianca asked with a sad look on her face.

"Yes, but if you were already on the plane, you should have gone straight there. Your bed on the plane is comfortable. All of this unnecessary traveling is wear and tear on the body."

"Do I tell you how to travel and the direction in which you should be traveling?" Sometimes Ricky made the craziest comments she thought.

"Honey, I'm sorry. I didn't mean to act like I didn't want to see you." He reached over and grabbed her hand. "Are you hungry?"

"Yes. Let's go to our favorite restaurant," said Bianca as they headed in the direction of Creations.

"How was the show and photo shoot?"

"It was tiring but it went well. I loved working with Eric Von. He understands me and I understand him," said Bianca.

"What does that mean?" Ricky inquired.

"He has photographed me on several occasions and I have always liked the magazine results."

"Is he the short brother with the Afro you introduced me to at the Grammy party last year?" asked Ricky.   He laughed and continued on.   "Is he the guy who came over and said the moment I started acting up, I'd better picture you two together?" He laughed harder with a burst of confidence.

"Yeah, that's crazy Eric," said Bianca.

"He is crazy to think he could take you from me," said Ricky as he stuck his chest out further.

"You'd better watch out!" Bianca joked. She took her shoes off and slid her feet over Ricky's legs while he was driving on the 10 freeway.

"Girl, you are going to make me pull over," Ricky said while rubbing her feet with his right hand and steering with his left.

"That may not be such a bad idea," she said tugging at his shirt.

"There are too many people on the freeway." He smiled.

"Not you – making excuses to not give me some! We have gotten busy on the freeway during rush hour, so don't try it." They both laughed.

CHAPTER 26
WEDDING DAY
BIANCA

Bianca and Mia were in Mia's bedroom at her house in Sherman Oaks. Bianca couldn't help but to beat herself up about not being able to make it to all of the rehearsals for Mia's wedding. She had made it to two, to be exact but Mia totally understood.

"Bianca, don't worry about it. You are here now. This is the most important day. I had your input as much as you could. Stop beating yourself up. Plus, girl, you paid for the caterer, flowers, limousine, videographer, and hired the best photographer in town. I'm not mad at you."

"Girl, you are here," said Portia.

"When you are a mega superstar, you can't be everywhere at once. You are here right now. This is the important day," said Veromica.

Bianca realized she should not have been bugging because this was not her day "Okay, I'll stop tripping. You all are right. Mia, you are such a beautiful bride." Bianca handed her a beautiful seven-karat diamond bracelet as the *something borrowed* traditional part of weddings. She picked seven because it meant the day of rest. Mia loved it so much she told her to keep it. "Later for traditions, your wedding is whatever you make it."

"Mia, you look stunning. I can't stop crying," said Portia.

"Well you better because you are making me mess up my makeup." Everyone laughed.

"Are you nervous?"

"Actually, I'm not as nervous as I thought I would be. I think my mom has taken all of my nerves and swallowed them. However, I'm starting to feel a little lightheaded."

They rushed to her.

"Have a seat young lady to cool your nerves," said Portia. Mia sat down at her vanity. Veromica positioned the fan towards her. Bianca started rubbing her back.

"Just breathe, girl. You are a little overwhelmed right now. It will pass in a couple of minutes."

Gina, Mia's mom knocked on the open door. "The limo is outside waiting, ladies. It's time."

Mia said she felt better and stood up. A big ripping sound echoed through the room. Mia had stepped on a portion of her dress while trying to stand up.

"Mommy, my dress is ruined," she cried. Everyone was stunned. Ms. Johnson ran over to Mia and held her daughter closely, while rubbing her back.

"Baby, it's okay. Don't worry, we'll fix it. Stop crying and let me see where the rip is. I'm sure it's not as bad as it sounded."

"Things happen like this on everyone's wedding day, Mia. We'll fix it," said Portia.

"Why did she say that?" Mia cried even harder.

"Mia, it's not that bad. I can't even see where you ripped the dress." Bianca kept pulling up the layers.

"I'm going to be late for my wedding." Mia cried harder.

"We're still trying to locate the rip. Mia sweetie, that should be the least of your worries. They will wait."

"But…." Said Mia.

"We know you don't like to be late for anything," said Veromica and Portia. "This is a good excuse."

"Is everything all right?" Mia's soon to be mother-in-law walked in the room.

"Yes, everything is fine," Bianca replied calmly. Mia's mother-in-law and Thomas's little sister walked into the room. Wow, they are going to be a beautiful family. Mia, her mother-in-law, and Nicky, Thomas's sister fit right into Mia's beautiful family. With their high cheekbones and picture frame smiles, they could also be a part of Bianca's family.

"It is only going to take five minutes to stitch," said Mia's mother-in-law.

Mia smiled and looked up at the ceiling. "There is a GOD."

Mia's grandmother walked in. "I'm so happy I have lived to see the day for one of my girls to get married. She always considered Bianca one of her daughters. "Mia, you look stunning. Every time I leave the room for a second and come back, you look better and better. Thomas is a lucky man."

"I am too, Grandmother," said Mia.

"Okay ladies, let's go," said Mia's Grandmother. "We don't want to be late getting to the church."

They walked towards the door. Mia ran back and looked in the mirror.

"Damn, I look good!" She quickly got over her ordeal.

"You sure do, all of the women told her." They left the house, piled into the stretch white Rolls Royce limousine and headed down to the First Baptist Church.

The sky was clear and the sun was shining bright. Bianca was happy it was a nice day for Mia. The bridal party wore Gucci sunglasses with a brownish tint that Bianca purchased from Italy, while on tour, that perfectly matched their burnt orange colored dresses. Mia's dress was absolutely divine. Bianca couldn't believe she had gotten it from Saks Fifth Avenue. Bianca suggested the specialty selection at Bergdolf. Thomas' mom was shopping at a customer appreciation sale early one Saturday and decided to take a look at the wedding dresses. She said it was $40,000, marked down by fifty percent, with an additional twenty-five percent off. Added to all of that was a fifteen-percent-off coupon she had received in the mail. She was psyched. She called Mia and told her to wake up because she had a surprise for her and she'd better like it! She was kidding about the 'she'd better like it part!' Surprisingly, Mia loved it. She was so grateful.

With minor alterations, the beautifully designed, Vera Wang, sleeveless, fitted v-back white dress was perfect. The dress came down just enough to cover Mia's white thin-strapped Manolo Blahnik shoes. Bianca was so happy to have picked those, because the picture of the Dolce & Gabbana shoes Mia had emailed her didn't flow with her theme. Bianca loved D&G but the shoes weren't a perfect match. There was one long pleat in the back of Mia's dress with a thin strip of burnt orange material underneath. It was very minute. No one would see that part of the dress until the reception, when she detached the 20-foot-long train from her gown. Bianca had brought it back from Milan after one of her tours. She had thought she would use it for her own wedding but since Mia was getting married first, it was only right that she pass it on to her.

The décor was of white and orange flower arrangements strategically placed on the inner sides of each pew. The church smelled like a million-dollar rose garden.

No one, except for the wedding party, was allowed to walk in the inside aisles. They had to get to their respective sides entering on the outside of the pews. Mia felt it would be bad luck for anyone unaffiliated with her actual wedding to walk in the space prior to her marriage being consecrated.

Mia's walk exuded sexiness. Her face glowed like that of a princess being captured by her knight in shining armor.

As Bianca stood watching Mia walk down the aisle with young handsome ushers behind her carrying her train, she thought *wow, what a joyous day.* Thomas, dressed in a tailored white Brioni suit, looked like a Calvin Klein model. Bianca tried not to cry. She stared at Ricky who was in the second row on the bride's side. Bianca wanted this day to become a reality for her too. Ricky smiled at her. She briefly glanced down the rows to check out the guests. She saw her parents who had flown in for the day. Her siblings were unable to make it, due to other commitments. She suspected her Dad had told her Mom it was not an option for them to sit next to Ricky. Bianca was certain her mom probably agreed, for the sake of an argument. Bianca waited for her cue to step out of line to sing the song, *Soul Mates By Definition of Love,* which she had written for the two lovebirds.

We stand before God
Our family and friends
A vow to love each other through thick and thin
As each day passes we shall always be one
Until the last hour of the setting sun
I love you more than ever before
Together we shall walk through that open door

Chorus:
Soulmates by definition of love
God has placed you in my world
I'll be there for you
Because you complete me
Together we're one
On a spiritual journey
Soulmates by definition of love

A love like two birds chirping in a tree
Storming rainy days, just you and me
Together forever a sense of serenity
Taking it back to the days of
Jumping the broomstick
Love is deep isn't it!
Because we're soulmates by definition of love

(Repeat chorus)

Two hearts connected as one
Joined together through love and devotion
How beautiful we are together
Slow walks in the park
Long talks in the dark
Loving one on one forever.

(Repeat chorus)

At peace I am with he.
A match made in heaven so wonderful as thee.
I'm here for you and you for me
Loving you has made my life change
Eternally yours, best friends for life
I thank you God for my beautiful wife

Upon completion of the song, all of the women and the groom were in tears. Even the groomsmen had a hard time holding back. It was magical. Bianca walked back to her place in the line-up while Reverend George Tenzer told Thomas and Mia to step forward. Mia walked over to light a white candle symbolizing her father's spiritual presence. She then immediately walked back over to stand next to Thomas. Reverend Tenzer was a distinguished, handsome deep dark man with salt and pepper wavy hair. He was 5'10" and wore a black suit with a white cardboard-like collar. He had the presence of Harry Belafonte. Mia grew up attending his church so the Reverend was able to talk about how beautiful a person inside, and out, she had become. He then introduced the next page of this storybook wedding.

"Please bring forth the sugar," said Reverend Tenzer. The best man and Bianca handed him the sugar in two small Tiffany pouches. Reverend Tenzer then placed the contents on a black cloth draped over the clear podium. He mixed the contents onto the cloth as he emptied it to symbolize them becoming one. Now it was time for the reading of the vows. Thomas and Mia faced each other. Bianca handed Mia her small white piece of paper as she spoke first.

"Thomas, you're the carrots of my eyes. The wings that make me fly. I stand before you as God and our guests are my witness to say, I will give you everything I have. I will walk beside you as my husband. May we be as happy as we are today, for the rest of our lives. I love you with all of my heart." Mia's voice was choppy by the end of her vows. She had tears bunched up between her long fake eyelashes. Thomas braced himself and proceeded to speak from his heart.

"Mia, you're my rock. I have always loved you. You're my best friend and will be forever. I look forward to spending the rest of my life with you. I can't wait to start a family with you." There were whimpers coming from the audience. Bianca turned to the audience and jokingly told everyone to stop crying. Everyone laughed including Thomas. Bianca jokingly instructed him to finish. Thomas tried to hold his composure in between his nervous laughter.

"You're my heart, my breath and my world. I love you," he said. Except for the sound of joyful tears from Mia, there was a few seconds of silence. She then fanned herself to help lighten up the moment.

"Oh my goodness, I said I wasn't going to cry anymore. I can't stop the tears. I am going to need the make up stylist and a new dress from the nervous sweat!" said Mia. Everyone laughed.

"This is why I love her." Thomas wiped her tears with his thumb.

"On that note, is there anyone here today that would object to this marriage? If so, please stand and speak." The Reverend looked around the room. "If not, forever hold your peace." He smiled. Thomas, please put the ring on Mia's finger. Thomas placed the triangular shaped diamond ring gently on Mia's finger and looked into her eyes.

"Mia, please put the ring on Thomas's finger." Mia lovingly slid the matching diamond band on Thomas's left hand.

There was silence. "Isn't this beautiful?" The Reverend asked everyone.

"Yes, it is," agreed all the guests.

Bianca arranged for a Lexus Truck limousine to pick up her parents at 7:30 p.m., in time for them to catch a Red Eye because Supreme had to finish preparing for summer school finals. Ricky and Bianca were not able to stay until the end of the reception either, because they were leaving at seven a.m. Bianca still needed to pack clothes on her own and with her stylist.

Bianca was a little stressed about going out on the road again, but she knew she had to do it.

CHAPTER 27
PLAYA
RICKY

"Honey, I'm going to drop you off at home and I'll be back later. I have to go back by the studio to finish some last-minute edits."

"Ricky, I thought you did that weeks ago."

"I did, but we never finished. Look Bianca, are you going to start this again?" Ricky asked, sounding perturbed.

"Start what?" asked Bianca, frowning.

"The crazy questions," said Ricky.

Bianca took a deep breath. "Forget it." She was pissed.

"Thank you," snapped Ricky.

Ricky didn't feel like being bothered with her 21 questions. He didn't understand why she needed to know his every move. It was so annoying. He leaned over to kiss her goodbye when he got to her driveway. She moved away.

"I'm not going to respond to your behavior tonight. We had a beautiful day. Your best friend just got married, so why are you tripping?" asked Ricky.

"I just don't want to be kissed right now."

"Fine, do you want me to come over later? I still have to go home and pack my clothes?"

"I thought you packed?"

"Bianca, stop searching. I will be at your house later. The sooner you let me go, the earlier I can come back to your house."

"Whatever." She got out of the truck and slammed the door. She was always tripping. He couldn't believe women remembered everything you told them. He didn't remember telling her that in the first place. It was like she hoarded a memory bank in her head. Her head should be the size of a floor model television, if one judged her by the amount of information she stored. Ricky vowed to start writing down the things he told her. He wasn't lying to her this time. He did have some studio business to take care of and it couldn't wait until he got back.

Ricky got a text message on his pager from Scooter.

What's up man? Where are you? This party is off the hook! You were supposed to be here two hours ago. You are always late. Hit me on the hip if you are coming. Scooter's message read across his screen. He had forgotten about Tyrone's party. He figured he would stop by for a half an hour. *I'm on my way kid.* He texted messaged him back while swerving on the freeway. Ricky made a U-turn and got onto the 10 freeway going west. "I'll be there in thirty minutes," he left a message on Scooter's cell.

Look at all these cars, he thought. He found parking, then got out and walked three blocks to the crème stucco house that took up the entire corner on Bradford Street in Beverly Hills. The door was open. Ricky walked in.

"It's about time you got here." Scooter walked up to him and slapped him five.

"Nice to see you, too. This must be *everyone yell at Ricky day!*" Ricky had a smirk on his face. "Honestly I had forgotten about the party. I was going to the studio for a little while, go home, pack my clothes and go back to Bianca's."

"How was the wedding?"

"It was cool. Mia looked fine as hell," said Ricky.

"Does that mean you want to sleep with Mia now?" Scooter asked sarcastically.

They both laughed.

"Maybe I already did," Ricky jokingly said.

"I don't think so."

"I'm playing. Thomas actually had tears coming out of his eyes. He's cool, but he is such a punk."

"The brother was just happy. Mia is fine and she can cook," said Scooter. "Sisters aren't trying to cook now-a-days. I would have cried, too. She's classy, fine and educated. Brothers can't find sane women like that anymore."

"Did they ever exist?" Ricky asked in a serious tone.

"Sure, we have met some really nice young ladies in our day. Bianca is nice."

"Whatever. She gets on my nerves. Since we're on the subject of women…" Ricky immediately got hyped when he saw all of the fine women walking around. "I see the women. Now where's the liquor?"

"The liquor is in the kitchen which is straight ahead to the right."

"That's all I needed to hear. I'll be back." Ricky squeezed through the crowd to go to the kitchen area.

"Hello Ricky."

"What's up, Princess?"

"You finally made it. I asked Scooter where you were."

"Yeah, I had a previous engagement to go to."

"Another party?" Here were the questions again. Women.

"Yeah, you can say that. I'll be right back." He didn't want to be bothered. "I'm getting myself and Scooter a drink."

"Take your time," said Princess.

Ricky went over to the homemade bar and requested a Heineken and a rum and Coke to act like he was getting Scooter one as well. As he turned around, he bumped into Simone, spilling some of his rum & Coke on her blouse.

"I'm so sorry." He put both drinks down and quickly got her a napkin. Simone wiped her blouse. "Can I get you anything?"

"No thanks, I changed my mind."

"Are you sure?" he asked.

"Yes, I'm sure," said Simone.

"Again, I'm sorry."

"It's okay. How are you? Do I get a hug?" asked Simone.

"Of course," said Ricky. They embraced each other like it was a movie scene.

"What's going on?"

"I just got back from New Orleans," she said.

"How was it?" he asked, suddenly remembering the phone call Bianca placed to her home, thank goodness while she was away.

"It was great. I was supposed to be there for a few months and ended up staying longer on set. How are you, Ricky?" she asked while seductively swaying.

"I'm great. I can't complain."

"You look great," said Simone.

"Thank you. You look nice also."

"I heard you and Bianca were back together."

"Who told you that?" asked Ricky.

"Word travels. You know how this industry is?"

"Speaking of industry; how is the industry treating you? I heard you were styling your butt off." He glanced at her breasts and then looked at her face and smiled. "It's going well. I can't complain either," she said.

"You are really looking good," Ricky's eyes wandered up and down her healthy thick body.

"Thank you."

"I'm sure you hear it often."

"You use to always say that to me."

"That's because it's true. Who are you here with?" Ricky asked as he took sneak peeks at her perky fake breasts.

"My girlfriends."

"Where are they?"

"On the dance floor."

"Where is your man?"

"I don't have a man."

"Why?" Ricky asked, knowing she didn't have a man because of her body language.

"I guess I haven't found anyone since you?"

"Are you lying to me?"

"No, it's true."

"That means I can take you out to dinner?"

Simone looked surprised. "What about Bianca?"

"Why are you asking me about Bianca? This conversation is between you and me. Bianca is not here."

"You never answered me as to whether you were dating her again."

"I'm dating her." Technically they weren't dating. They were boyfriend and girlfriend.

"Are you dating her or is she your girlfriend?"

"Why are you so preoccupied with Bianca? Why do women always have to have your relationship defined?" He finished the last of his beer.

"I don't want to go to dinner with you if you have a girlfriend."

He ignored her. "I have to go out of town tomorrow morning but I'll be back next week so pick a restaurant and leave the information on my answering machine."

"Why don't I call you at your hotel or are you going away with a girl?"

"This is about business. You know what I do. Also, I'm not sure which hotel they have me staying in. You can try me on my cell." He knew he would be out of the country and it would go straight to voicemail. He had one thing on his mind and that was having his way with Simone. Bianca had pissed him off and he didn't feel like arguing.

"Okay, I'll pick a place. Do you still have the same number?"

"Of course.

"I thought maybe you had gotten married," Ricky said lying again.

"I'm not checking for anyone like that. What about yourself?"

"What?"

"Marriage. Do you have someone in the winds that you'd like to marry?"

"Nope, I'm not getting married any time soon." He quickly thought about Bianca and the 50 times they had talked and fought about marriage. He finished the last of his second rum & Coke. "Hold that thought, I need another drink. Are you sure you don't want anything?"

"No," said Simone. You better slow down. This is your third drink since you've been talking to me. That is a lot for someone who has only been talking for an hour."

"Why are you counting all the drinks I have?" They flirted with each other. He imagined the positions he use to have her in.

"No reason. It's no big deal."

"No prospects?" asked Simone.

"Nope." He tried to keep a straight face.

"Does Bianca think she is a prospect?"

"Look, why are you sweating me about Bianca? Don't worry about her. She is not thinking about you. Can we move on to talking about what is going on after this party?" Ricky was puzzled and bothered by her fascination with Bianca.

"I'm not sure. Why? Do you know of something else going on?" asked Simone.

"I'm trying to hang out with you. What's up?" asked Ricky.

"Well, where do you want to go?"

"Anywhere you want to go. What about a walk along the beach?"

Walking was major booty points. This would really make a woman think he was the father of romanticism! He knew he really needed to call Bianca. He looked at his watch. It was almost two in the morning. He focused back to Simone. He didn't want to deal with Bianca's mouth.

"Excuse me for one second, I need to go outside and use my cell."

"No problem. I need to check on my girlfriends anyway."

"Let's meet back here in ten minutes."

"Sounds good."

He walked over to talk to Scooter who was talking to a girl. "Hey man, where have you been all night?" asked Scooter.

"Hi Denise. How are you?" asked Ricky.

"I'm fine. How are you?"

"Great. I can't complain. I know you all are talking. Scooter, I came over to tell you that I'm going outside for a minute, and then I'm leaving. I have to catch a plane in the morning."

"Okay." Scooter was totally not interested in what Ricky was saying. He turned around to go outside and call Bianca. He walked a little ways down the street in an attempt to cut out all of the background noise and music.

"Hello…" She was asleep.

"Hey B, I'm not going to be able to make it over there. I'm still at the studio and I have to go home to pack my clothes."

"Whatever Ricky, I can hear the loud music in the background," she sounded sleepy and annoyed that he woke her up and was lying. "You knew all of this before."

"Honey, don't act like this. I will meet you at the Airport Hanger in the morning."

"Okay, fine. Do whatever you have to do. I'll see you in the morning."

"Are you upset with me?"

"No, just sleepy," Bianca said while yawning.

"I'll make it up to you. I have to go because I'm finishing up on some last-minute things before I get out of here." Ricky knew she knew he wasn't telling the truth but at that point he didn't care. She had been acting like a witch since earlier in the evening and he was tired of it.

"Okay, I love you."

"I love you, too. See you in the morning." Bianca hung up without saying goodbye.

Simone walked over just as he ended the call.

"Hey, ten minutes turned into twenty minutes."

"I'm sorry. I stopped to talk to Scooter for a minute. I wanted to take you for a walk on the beach but it has gotten a little too late. I still have to get my things together for tomorrow and I have an early flight."

"That's cool. We can do it some other time."

"Do you want to keep me company while I pack my things?"

"Sure, but I don't think you should be driving, Ricky."

"I know."

"Well, I didn't drive my car. I rode with my girlfriends. Do you want me to drive?"

"Yes," Ricky sounded excited. He wanted to forget about Bianca even if it was for a few minutes.

"You can drop me off at home on your way to the airport."

"Cool. Let's do it."

"Let me go inside and tell my friends I'll see them later."

They walked down the block to his truck. He handed Simone the keys and she got in on the driver side while he climbed in on the passenger side. "Can you handle a truck?"

"Of course, I handled you," she said flirtatiously.

"Don't start anything you can't complete." Ricky, thankful for his tented windows, ran his fingers through her unusually long curly weave.

"You already started." She leaned over and kissed him on the lips. *It's on.* He smiled an intoxicated smile.

Ricky and Simone arrived at Ricky's house at Emerald Estates in Sherman Oaks, which was across from the Mercedes dealership. His home was dimly lit and he turned on the light as they entered the house.

"Your place is nice, Ricky. You got new furniture?" Simone asked while looking around.

"Yeah, a few months ago. I'm glad you like it."

Ricky staggered into his bedroom and immediately set his alarm for 5:15 a.m. He pulled his clothes from the closet, brought them into the living room and placed them on the couch.

Simone sat down on the black leather love seat adjacent to the matching couch.

"Do you want something to drink?"

"Yeah, what do you have?"

"Spring water, beer, orange juice, wine, and more wine."

"I'll take a glass of wine."

"Actually, you're not a guest. You know where the refrigerator is."

"I'll get it."

Simone went into the kitchen and got a glass of wine. She returned to the living room and sat down next to Ricky, who hit 'play' on the CD player. Soothing sounds from Milo David's jazz played in the background. Ricky turned to Simone and started kissing her passionately. She responded quickly and soon all of Ricky's clothes that he had placed on the couch fell to the floor. He gently laid her down while utilizing his tongue as if it were an animal on the prowl looking for food.

Simone slipped her hands up Ricky's shirt and caressed his chest. She then attempted to move her hands down to his belt buckle.

"Hold on a minute." He stumbled to get up and take his clothes off. Simone took her red BCBG tank top off and Ricky reached down to take her short black skirt off, then peeled her underwear off with his mouth.

"Are you ready?" Ricky asked her as he fumbled to get his condom on and slowly entered Simone.

He forgot how loud of a moaner she was. It was okay because it was good for his ego. "Ricky, you are still the bomb."

"So are you."

"Does this mean we are going to start dating again?" asked Simone with a pleased look on her face.

"Anything is possible," he said caught up in the moment.

"Well, at least you didn't say no." She was relieved.

"Shhhhhh," said Ricky.

They both moaned for what seemed like hours. Simone moved Ricky around and got on top. He loved an aggressive woman. "Girl, you are putting it on me."

"Is that a good thing?"

"Hell, yeah. Not too many women can make my toes curl!"

Sweat was pouring off of them, their lips smacked against each other loudly. Their bodies sounded like wet bathing suits being elasticized.

"Ricky, I missed this. I missed you too."

He slapped her butt to show her the booty was getting *real* good. He slowly turned her body around and got on top.

"Ahh Ricky. Why can't I have this on a daily basis?"

He ignored her and continued to pump. Bianca's face flashed in his mind. He dismissed it immediately. She had pissed him off.

"Ohhhhhhhhh sweetieeeeeeeeeee, you are screwing the hell out of me."

Ricky let out a loud roaring moan and then collapsed onto Simone's limp body.   They both lay there breathing heavily. Ricky rolled over and looked at the clock on top of his entertainment center. Shit, it was 4:00 a.m.!

"I'd better get up and finish packing! Do you want a towel to take a shower?"

"Yes, please." Simone was still somewhat out of breath.

"Thanks for keeping me company while I *packed my clothes*, Simone." They pulled up to her luxury apartment complex in Culver City.

"Are we still going to go to dinner when you get back?" Simone pleaded.

"I'm going to try." Ricky answered uninterested.

"Before, it was a done deal. Now that we slept together, you seem a little hesitant about our date."

"That's not true. You know I'm a busy man. I'm really going to try."

"Okay Ricky, I see that you are up to your same tricks again."

"Simone, look, I can't argue with you right now. I have a plane to catch. I don't know why you are tripping. I'm going to call you when I return."

"What about dinner?" asked Simone adamantly.

"We will go to dinner. I will call you as soon as I land in Chicago."

Ricky knew he wasn't going to call her when he got to Chicago. Heck, he thought, he wasn't even going to Chicago! He wanted her to get the heck out of his truck immediately.

"Okay, have a safe flight. I'll speak to you later."

"Yeah, yeah, yeah." He was trying to focus on getting to the Airport Hanger to meet Bianca for the seven a.m. flight to Africa. He had lied to Simone about the destination because Bianca had been on several television stations and announced she would be performing in Africa. He didn't want her to start another conversation based on that.

CHAPTER 28
TOUR
BIANCA

Wow, the band was there and everyone else was on time as well. Bianca was so surprised. She had set up an emergency meeting with the staff and crew prior to the trip explaining to them the significance of them being on time. She didn't play that late mess.

"Good morning," Bianca said forgetting she was disappointed with Ricky.

"Good morning," said Ricky.

"How was your evening last night? Did you get everything accomplished that you wanted?" Bianca asked coyly.

"Yes, of course. I didn't get to bed until early this morning. I got out of the studio really late and then had to pack my clothes."

"Yeah, right." Bianca said pushing her mouth to one side to show she knew he was being dishonest. "Why didn't you kiss me when you saw me?" She complained.

"Are you going to start tripping? Why didn't you kiss me when you saw me?" Ricky asked.

"Come here. Ricky walked over to Bianca and kissed her on the cheek. "It would be nice to kiss my boyfriend on the lips." She kissed him on the lips and slyly slid her tongue into his mouth. Ricky responded with a smile. "Good, we're boarding. Do you have your paper work?"

"Yeah, it's in my briefcase," Ricky answered.

"Hi, Miss Baxter, we're ready to board," said Onree, the flight attendant.

"Sweetie, let's go." She told the band members and the rest of the crew that she would see them on the plane. She and Ricky walked past them and boarded the plane.

"Being on the road is tiresome." She was on a three-way call complaining to Mia and her mom while in the hotel room. "I'm sick of living out of suitcases."

"Well, honey, you have to wait it out. Sometimes we don't like a portion of what our jobs require, but we have to stick it out," said Supreme.

"Just enjoy it," said Mia.

"I'm trying. Maybe if my man was acting right, I'd be able to enjoy the road a little more."

"Well..." said Mia.

Bianca interrupted her. "But I don't want to talk about him. I'm going to lie down and get some rest. I have a hectic day tomorrow and I have jet lag. Mia, I'm glad that your honeymoon went wonderfully."

"Okay, sweetie, get some rest," said Supreme. Remember, God does not put things upon us in which we can not bear."

"I know that's right," said Mia.

"Yeah Mom, you did always say that. I love you both."

"I love you too, honey."

"Love ya back, B. Hang in there, girl. You are a Baxter," Mia said in a deep raspy voice imitating Mr. Baxter.

"That's what Daddy always said." Everyone laughed as they said bye and hung up the phone. Bianca took a shower and fell asleep as soon as her head hit the pillow. She woke up to find Ricky all cuddled up under her. She tried to slide his arm off of her and gently put his leg back on his side of the bed. He awakened.

"Hi baby."

"Good afternoon."

"Afternoon? Where are you going?"

"I'm going to the bathroom. Do you mind?" Bianca asked with a stink attitude.

"My, you are grouchy today," Ricky said in between yawns. "You went to bed early, huh?"

"Yeah, I was tired."

"I'm starving so I'm going downstairs for some lunch.

"I'm going back to sleep." Ricky stretched his legs across the entire bed and put the pillow over his head. She turned on the shower.

Bianca loved Africa. She felt blacks hadn't truly lived until they had experienced a trip to the motherland. When they walked out of the small dusty airport it seemed like all of Africa were standing there ready to greet them. It was like a block party. They had the tambourines going, the beating of the drums, the singing, dancing and shouting. They were so moved. She handed Ricky her bags and joined in with them. They had a big banner that said, *Welcome Home My Brothers and Sisters.* They also had posters from her first album. They were a little behind in times but it didn't matter. They shouted Bianca's name and sang her first hit song with their strong accent. It was amazing.

There were also some that hounded her for money or for whatever she could give them. The first time she went she didn't know what to expect. This was her fourth time in Africa and she was prepared. She brought posters, lipstick and nail polish for the ladies, gum and stickers for the children, tee shirts and $300.00 in one dollar bills for the men. They really loved black tee shirts. She would spend a few hours in the morning on some of her days visiting schools. Bianca took a particular liking to one fourth grade classroom because the children were extremely bright, especially the cute little brown girl that inquired, through an interpreter, about presidential issues going on in the United States. A charming little boy wanted to know what Americans really thought atbout African people in the motherland. Bianca was sad to see that the respectful students had to share pencils and barely had enough paper. She decided she would send the school $50,000 a month if they promised not to convey it to the media.

The food was the most incredible food she had ever tasted. It was chemical free. The chicken wasn't fattened up. It was the size of a U.S. hen. The vegetables were large and tasty. She wanted to bring some back to the States. After eating herself into a frenzy she went back upstairs to lie down for a few more hours. Her show was at 8:00 p.m.

Sunset Sahel was the hottest club in Dakar, Senegal. It was really hip in an early 90's kind of way. They went through the back entrance and they were playing a song from Negative's second album. She could hear the crowd. They were pumped up.

It was such an amazing experience. Although another popular artist named Bizbust had had a few Rap albums under his belt, the crowd was still rocking hits from his first album. Ricky and Bianca sat in a 200-square-foot room, while she drank her bottled water and meditated for ten minutes, as she always did before a performance. Then, it was time for her to do what she did best.

"What's up, Dakar? You are beautiful. My beautiful black people. I'm so honored to be here. You all always show me loveeeeeee."

The crowd got louder with each verse she sang. When she started to sing songs from her first album, they went crazy. She didn't want to break up the fast music flow so she came out wearing a fitted Tarzan outfit and sang "RUN WILD," an up-tempo song.

After a few songs from the first and second album, she slowed it down and made a smooth transition into her second album, then third. She wasn't surprised at the response because she was told it was being played on the radio and the remix with Negative was already in the clubs. Some closed their eyes and seemed to be in heavy thoughts while following along to "LOVING HIM UNCONDITIONALLY," the most popular single of her first two albums. Every time she sang this song, she wanted to cry. She looked into the audience and truly felt at home. She started off by asking if anyone had been in love and gotten hurt.

"By a show of hands, who has given their all and felt unappreciated? Who has loved someone unconditionally?" It works in every city. The guys and girls put their hands up. There was a little chatter until she hit that first note.

She held the mic in one hand and extended her other arm towards the crowd. "Sing along with me if you know this song."

It's me who blessed you with my love
It's time we decided to end this charade
We don't talk like we used to.
All we do is fight fight fight

Change is good, wouldn't you say?
Why do people play this love game?
Why is it so hard to break from you?
Being with you I feel lonely too
The weakness in me wants to spend the night
This time it just ain't right

When we met it was heaven on earth
The dates were great and you weren't a jerk
We met the families and was accepted within
The love part came and you got scared
You ran from me but there was a wall
So you didn't get far.

Let's get in our cars and drive in separate directions.
You beat me once, twice, three times.
Next you'll kill me.
You already have destroyed my body!

The breeze that floats through my mind
Stops in the midst
I need to change environments and the man I'm with
We're great people, just not together
I have to move on this time forever!

"We love you, Bianca," a man yelled from the crowd in his heavy accented voice.

"I love you, too." She felt a sense of peace and strength. Singing took her out of reality and put her mind at ease. While doing her last song, she jumped down with her security guys and went through the crowd. This was always magical.

"Thank you all for showing me so much love, Senegal. As always, it has been great. I love you all. Have a good night."

The sweat was pouring off of her face. She was handed a bottle of water.

When they returned to the Sofitel Hotel, she was wiped-out. After a warm shower, she conked out on the bed. She was still tired the next morning but promised Ricky and the band that she would go with them to see a historical site on their day off. She had put it off several times before. She thought it would be too much for her to handle.

As they took the ride to The Point Of No Return, she was filled with emotion. It was almost like anxiety was taking over her body. As they approached this large, pinkish Victorian home, she started to feel the presence of her ancestors. Ricky had been here several times before and wanted her to see it with him for their first time. Unfortunately, that didn't happen, but she was glad she was finally seeing it, even though they had company. Their guide was a tall, slender, seventy-year old African with the bone structure of Nelson Mandela. They followed him up the beautiful wide spiral staircase to where slave masters once lived. The spacious rooms were heavily decorated and the furniture was a gorgeous, antique style.

As they descended down another magnificent staircase painted in a pretty, pale pink, they entered into sections where the slaves had lived. There were holding cells where hundreds of Africans at a time had been kept. Only the size of four outhouses squared in front of each other, it made Bianca cringe. They looked like dungeons. The rooms were made out of rocks and the rock ceilings were approximately five-by-seven. There were no doors. As they walked down through this awful place, they passed by the infant and children's room located on the left side. Diagonally across was the women's room and diagonally to that was the men's dungeon. As they continued walking, she stopped in her tracks.

"As you can see, there is a small door just up ahead facing the ocean. That is the POINT OF NO RETURN. This was the door where Africans went through to board a ship and never to return to their families," said the guide.

As Bianca proceeded forward, tears started in the corners of her eyes. She got to the door and stared into the outside air. Ahead of her were miles and miles of water. Below her were white and tan rocks. She stepped out into the breezy air. She told Ricky she wanted to be alone for a moment. He understood. She knew this was a place one had to build up courage to attend. She sat down on a large rock and went into meditation mode. She sobbed for what seemed like hours. She sobbed for her ancestors. She sobbed for their innocence and her ignorance. She uttered words as a tribute in between the huge tears flowing down her face and dripping into her mouth.

> *God almighty, strong beautiful black man above*
> *Humble me with honesty, integrity and love.*
> *Make me never forget this day*
> *When I go back to the States so far away.*
> *My people have made it possible for me...*
> *Possible to voice my talents graciously.*
> *To feel their love and know their pain*
> *Is enough to make me go insane.*
> *To know myself is to know my past.*
> *Black is beautiful inside and out*
> *So this is what I'm really about.*

As she stared out into the ocean through her cloudy eyes, she kept asking herself why. She tried to imagine living back then. Living in a world where one was beaten because of the color of their skin. They were verbally, mentally, emotionally and spiritually desecrated.

"Bianca, are you all right?" Ricky tapped her on the shoulder and startled her.

"Hi sweetie, I'm fine." She looked up at Ricky through her teary eyes. "We have been blessed, huh?" He stared out into the water. She got up. "I'm sorry. I had to sit here and reflect."

"It's okay. I came to make sure you were okay. You've been out here for about forty-five minutes and everyone is getting hungry. Plus, they want to see Goree Island and Pink Lake before it gets too late."

"I'm coming," Bianca said with sorrowed hollow eyes.

Ricky put his arm around her and pulled her close. He wiped the remaining tears from her eyes. "Give me one second."

"I know your seconds," Ricky said as he smiled while trying to lighten up the mood."

She smiled back as she pulled out her small compact and quickly touched up her face. "There, now do I look decent?" She turned and looked at him.

"You look beautiful as always," he said in a tone without any feeling. He looked somewhat annoyed.

She walked ahead of him. They entered the house through the entrance of the Point of No Return. This time Bianca didn't look into the rooms. She kept her eyes focused on the front entrance. As she got close, she could hear the voices of another group. They weren't speaking English. She continued to hurriedly approach the front entrance. Smiling was not an option right now. Later for the protocol.

"Are you okay, Bianca?" asked the band members and background singers as they walked through the little town stopping to look at the African crafts.

"I'm fine. I was just taken aback by the magnitude of what we saw. Sorry, I know you all are hungry. Let's eat."

"Cool," said Ricky as he grabbed her hand. She wanted to eat back at her favorite restaurant, V.S.D. Vendredi (Friday), Samedi (Saturday), and Dimanche (Sunday). It's only open on the weekends.

Goree Island was beautiful. Pink Lake was stunning. The Lake was actually a rosy pink color. Bianca wanted to jump in. However, they were told not to go into the lakes or the ocean.

"Wow, I have never seen anything like this."

"Isn't this great?" asked Ricky.

From there, they got in an open truck and took the road to a village where they met a King who had four wives. It was a trip. He was a fine, seven foot tall, African man with skin as smooth as a chocolate bar. He must have had about fifteen kids. They were beautiful. They favored Ethiopian people but two shades darker. They were so happy to see Bianca. One little girl she wanted to take home. She was about four. She kept staring at Bianca and touching her face. He showed them where everyone slept. Bianca, of course, had to go to the bathroom and forgot where she was. This wasn't going to be easy! She had to plant her feet into the smooth sand behind a bamboo hut, after she found a dry spot to squat! That was truly an experience she wanted to forget!

They then ventured into a town that sold gifts. She purchased Mia a little gift for her graduation.

The day was long but intriguing. It made Bianca appreciate her blackness more. By the time they got back to the hotel, most of them were exhausted. She could barely make it into the shower. Ricky and a few band members decided to go out to one of the clubs.

"Honey, we're leaving in the morning."

"I know. I can hang."

"Okay, Mr. Hang, please pack our belongings before you leave since you can hang and you have so much energy!"

"No problem."

Bianca tried to stay up and watch television but she was slowly falling asleep. She felt Ricky kiss her goodnight. The television ended up watching her. Ricky said when he came back to the room she was sprawled out over the entire bed!

"What do you mean, we can't leave? Ricky go and see what the problem is."

"Relax Bianca. They are saying that due to the weather they want us to wait."

"How long do they want us to wait?" asked Bianca disturbed by that statement. "Mia's graduation is in a couple of days." Bianca had on her battle face. She could feel her temper rising.

"I know, but I need you to relax. Would you prefer to fly and stand the risk of crashing? You are acting like a spoiled child right now," said Ricky adding to her fiery behavior.

"Whatever," Bianca started to raise her voice, immediately remembered where she was, then calmed down.

Ricky walked over to speak with the manager again.

"We might as well go back to the hotel." Ricky came back to Bianca and the band crew.

"What did they say? Should I talk to someone?" Bianca was prepared to take care of business.

"No, I handled it." He said annoyed by the entire situation. They were stuck for the next day and a half. Bianca's nerves were shot because all she thought about was missing Mia's graduation from UCLA Law School. Africa was great but she was more than ready to go home.

The ride back to the hotel was a quiet one. Ricky was right. Bianca inquired about the commercial flights to feel like she had tried 100%. They weren't letting any planes in or out of the country. There was nothing they could do so she decided they should make the best of a bad situation.

She had one of the African designers make her a lovely dress in a fabulous green fabric. A day and a half later they were on their way home. Her plane was still late getting out and it made Bianca a nervous because she was pushing it close trying to get home to Mia's graduation. Ricky had to go straight to an instore.

CHAPTER 29
GRADUATION
BIANCA

It was a good thing that she had purchased Mia's main gift in Africa. She had to go straight from the Airport Hangar. She picked up some flowers from a man selling them outside of UCLA. She arrived at the gymnasium just as they were calling Mia's name. "MIA RENEE ZANZ."

"Wooooooooooooooooo Mia, way to go." Bianca and her security ran down towards the stage. She was so happy for her.

She reached the first row in the aisle, put her bag down, and with tears in her eyes, continued to yell Mia's name. As Mia crossed the stage and everyone quieted down, she yelled again, "Do your thing, girl." It was clearly ghetto style but she didn't care. Mia looked, started crying and mouthed, "*you made it.*"

"Of course I made it, girl. I wouldn't miss this for the world."

The man conferring the degrees scooted Mia along. Mia walked back to her seat with tears of joy. *My best friend is here*, Bianca knew she was thinking. All eyes were on her.

"Hi Bianca," said some young girl.

"Damn, she is equally as fine in person," said a tall, handsome white guy with dirty blond hair and green eyes.

You are fine too, she thought to herself.

"Wow, look, there's Bianca Baxter!" shouted a redheaded woman in her thirties.

"It's Bianca from television," another woman pointed out.

Bianca smiled and remained focused on her best friend. She slowly made her way over to Mia's husband, family, and in-laws. "Hey everyone."

"We weren't sure if you were going to make it," said Thomas.

"Are you kidding? Miss my girl's graduation? Never." There was no need to let them know she had almost missed the graduation, Bianca thought.

"I'm glad you made it," said Gina, Mia's mom.

"That will conclude today's ceremony ladies and gentlemen, said the president of U.C.L.A. All may rise. The corny graduation music came on and all of the students threw their hats in the air. They walked out to the lobby area. She could hear Mia's big mouth rushing her way through the crowd. Thomas stepped forward to hand her a bouquet of beautiful roses. He hugged and kissed her tightly.

"I'm so proud of you honey."

"Thanks sweetie. I love you."

"I love you too." They hugged and kissed each other again. This time passionately.

"Oooooowwwww! Shouted their surrounding family and friends.

"He's my husband." Mia looked up, took a prissy bow, and walked over to Bianca.

"Girl, I was sad because I thought you weren't coming."

"If I had to walk here, I was coming," said Bianca. Everyone laughed.

"I'm so glad you made it," admitted Mia.

"Congratulations." Bianca handed her the flowers and her gift.

"Thanks, girl. You didn't have to bring me anything. Just yourself."

"Mia, I'm truly proud of you. I love ya, girl."

"I love you, too." They both said as their eyes watered.

"You two are so emotional," said Mia's mom.

People were constantly walking up to Bianca asking for her autograph. A line developed. *"I haven't mastered the understanding of invasion of privacy,"* she mumbled. She continued to smile at her fans while they took pictures with loved ones while also trying to ignore the groupies.

Thomas stepped forward. "I'll handle this." He addressed the crowd who had gathered.

"Ladies and Gentlemen, I'm Bianca Baxter's Manager. No disrespect but Bianca is here on behalf of her best friend's graduation. She loves each and every one of you as fans and appreciates all of your support, but please try and understand.

Being that you are loyal fans you are probably aware that she has been on a long, extensive tour and would like to now spend some quality time with her close friends. Please respect her privacy at this time. No pictures or autographs."

Everyone was stunned and excited at the same time.

"Thomas is amazing. He was an actor in another life," Gina whispered to the both of them. Mia smiled, proud of her new hubby taking charge of the situation.

"Can we go now? There's too many people standing here and I'm hungry," said Grandma.

"Grandma, you are such a snob." Mia hugged her.

"We're waiting for my in-laws. They went to the rest room. You know Mr. Zanz has to go everywhere Mrs. Zanz goes," said Mia.

"Here they come," said Thomas.

"We're back," said Mrs. Zanz. Did we miss anything?"

"Nothing worth talking about," said Thomas. They were such a cute couple. They reminded Bianca of a younger version of Ozzie Davis and Ruby Dee.

The people had dispersed. However there were stragglers passing by and whispering to each other... "Did you see her?" "She is more beautiful in person."

They were finally able to get everyone together and leave. Thomas threw a party for Mia at their house and the food was catered by a new restaurant that a co-worker told him about. They had a wonderful evening. Bianca started to reflect on how wonderful Mia's life had turned out. She was very happy for her best friend.

CHAPTER 30
TOUR CONTINUED
BIANCA

   The latter part of the tour was going great. Bianca wasn't sure if it was because it was almost over or if they were truly having a great time. She complained a lot about being on the road but there is truly nothing like traveling, seeing the world, and experiencing various cultures, especially in her plane. She felt this world was amazing. Performing in Denver, Colorado was always fun in the early days, especially seeing the guys with their string ties and cowboy hats! She remembered going skiing one year in Vail with Ricky and the band members on one of her days off. She tried to get Ricky to *actually* join her on the slopes but the Brooklyn in him came out real quick. He let her know he preferred the water sports and it wasn't up for discussion or debate!

   Performing in Las Vegas was always fun with all of the glitter and gaudiness. The band always wanted to stay at the Venetian but Bianca loved the ambiance of Caesars Palace. At the Venetian, there was way too much gold in one setting for her! She was fine with the Palace and it's impeccable service.

   Washington D.C. always gave her love. Chocolate City had the finest African- American men in the world. They came out in packs to see her. She felt like this city was the easiest to get around, and the most exiting.

   Atlanta was another Chocolate City where she received lots of love. It always amazed her. She was supposed to do two intimate shows at the Fox Theatre. Tickets went on sale at 10:00 am and were sold out by 10:15 am. They wound up adding another show. She felt bad because tickets were sold out within 15 minutes as well and there was no way they could add another show, for she had to move on to the next city.

   Arco Arena in Sacramento was fun because aside from Sac having the Sacramento Kings, there wasn't much else going on. The people seemed bored and content. Therefore, they came out in masses. She had a crazy experience this time around. A guy in the front row was pointing at her and trying to give the security guard a piece of paper to pass to her. She wasn't quite sure where his lady friend, girlfriend, wife or whomever he was with, was during this process. All of a sudden Bianca saw a woman's hand connect with his face and it didn't look good. By the time she had worked her way back over to the left side of the stage, passing the props, a pink art deco living room scene, security was forcefully escorting them out.

She had a different experience in every city including Connecticut, Portland, Dallas, Houston, San Diego, New Jersey, etc. She loved Oakland because it reminded her of New York City, it had its own flavor. Oakland generated some of the coolest artists and musicians in music history, and some of the most prominent homes of independent artists.

In all of Bianca's travels, her most memorable city was always Detroit, home of Motown's Hitsville U.S.A., and respected home to the most talented African American artists, writers, and musicians to ever walk this earth. Performing at their Fox Theatre always made Bianca's imagination think of the Motown days. In Detroit's most historical building Bianca always came alive. She actually felt the presence of the great singers who were before her. Ricky said Bianca should perform in every city as if she were in Detroit. Her fans wouldn't recognize the difference because the majority of them were not on her tours throughout the entire leg. However, she did have some die-hard fans that went from city to city wearing tee shirts with her face on the front and FAN CLUB on the back. She often had her assistant interact with them via email. These fan club presidents could be scary at times. She loved her fans but some of them had obsessive behaviors. Every time Bianca visited Detroit she went to Berry Gordy's creation to get rejuvenated. She didn't have to take the tour. She simply walked through the house as if she lived there. Upon entering the small house, there was a long corridor with beautiful black and white and colored pictures of the Jackson 5, Diana Ross, Smokey Robinson & the Miracles, Marvin Gaye, and Aretha Franklin, to name a few. Berry had once lived in a section of the house and the house still had the original dishes he used. The candy machine was right before you entered into the studio with Stevie Wonders favorite candy bar connected to the #3 pull out knob. The studio was amazing. Bianca actually played the piano that Stevie played and sang a Motown song for a church group visiting from Arkansas. Ricky was mad at her because she was set to perform in four hours. The fans had asked and she felt compelled to comply. Overall there had been a little drama but nothing unusual. Bianca knew not to sing all out and blow out her voice. She simply wanted to give her fans a little taste.

One of her background singers had a falling out with one of the band members because she caught him in the car screwing some little groupie girl. Bianca heard about it at sound check when she quit. She told the singer if she quit on the spot, she would not pay for her ticket back to L.A. The singer was cool with that. She was told to vacate the hotel room as well. Bianca had no thoughts about it one way or the other. It was about business. She always kept three background singers because one never knew what could happen on the road. They could wing it with two girls for a night but she didn't want to do it any longer. She told her assistant to fly a girl named Naomi to Phoenix by tomorrow morning. They had two free days so it was not a big deal.

Hindsight was always a trip because Bianca subconsciously had suspected a little tension with the singer and band member in Africa, but she was always so tired she didn't really pay attention to it. There was a little batting of the eyes the day before at sound check and during the actual performance. She didn't know what was up but as long as it didn't interfere with their performance, she didn't care.

At a 24-hour diner in Virgina, she was still struggling with the fact that they were there such a late hour. She kept thinking she should have gone back to the hotel like the singers usually decided to do. She always eased her conscience by having a fruit cup and herbal tea. Of course the band members opted to have pancakes stacked a mile high.

On her day off she had a 2:30 a.m. wake-up call and a driver to take her to the Sedona Retreat and Healing Center. The unpaved gravel road was ten miles long and it was very dark. The Korean Master and Bianca went up to the top of the red-brick-looking mountain and through meditation and tai chi, they watched the sunrise.

She felt so relaxed and serene. She noticed it in her performance that night. Touring the West Coast and seeing and appreciating God's beauty was always a plus for her. After touring from Coast to Coast she was so happy to go back to Phoenix. When she initially saw the itinerary she was upset because she couldn't understand why they were backtracking, but she wanted to sing at Radio Magic's funeral. He lasted much longer than he thought. God was good.

Ricky and Bianca flew to the Grand Canyon and took a private helicopter ride to the bottom. She was scared to death. They had been to the Grand Canyon before but never in a helicopter. "See what alcohol will do to you!" She teased Ricky. She kept telling the pilot to slow down. He was very patient with her. Ricky kept telling her to relax because she was missing the beauty of the ride. Finally they got down to the bottom. She took many deep breaths and drank lots of water. It was amazing.

The colors of the flowers were magnified. They saw butterflies and she wanted to jump out and take a bite out of the plants. They were so green. The rocks that had broken off from the mountains looked beautiful.

"Okay Ricky, you're right, it's incredible."

"I thought I was going to have to give you a tranquilizer," said the pilot.

"I thought we were going to have to push her out," said Ricky. They laughed.

"I know I've probably been your worst passenger."

"No, the most important part was that you were able to eventually relax," said the pilot.

"Honey, look at that," said Ricky.

"Wow, these mountains are different colors over here. Green, yellow, cream, and red. The last time we were here we started walking down to the bottom of the Grand Canyon."

"You started? Did you make it down to the bottom?" asked the pilot.

"Of course not! She complained of being too hot," said Ricky.

"That is so not true!"

"What was your excuse?" They laughed.

"I didn't realize the trail was so steep. Between maintaining your balance and dodging the large doo-doo balls from the mules, I became overwhelmed."

By this time the pilot was laughing really hard. "Miss Baxter, if someone would have told me you were this funny I would not have believed them."

"I keep telling her she's not adventurous."

"It was way too hot."

"It gets hotter the further you walk down the Canyon," said the pilot.

"Man, she kept saying, honey, did you forget we have to walk back up the mountain? I kept telling her that we hadn't walked down far enough to be concerned about the walk back up."

Ricky was clapping his hands and laughing. "Oh now you are a comedian! Sir, what's your name again?"

She looked up at the front of his shirt. He was an older, white-haired man, kind of country looking. "My name is Peter."

"Peter, other people were passing us and listening to the conversation and looking at us like *what the heck is she talking about.*" They were still laughing as they got out of the helicopter.

"I have to tell you two, I have been doing this for seventeen years and this has been one of the most exciting rides for me."

"I'm glad," said Bianca. Ricky put his arm around Bianca and kissed her on the cheek. "Now you want to be affectionate." Ricky took out his wallet and handed Peter a one hundred dollar bill.

"You were excellent, man."

"Wow, are you sure you meant to give this to me, sir?"

"That statement alone is the reason why you deserve it." Bianca shook Peter's hand.

"In other parts of the country some people would have thought it was a mistake and stuck the money in their pockets," said Ricky.

"Really."

"Thanks so much for a wonderful time, Peter. It was great. Take care." Bianca and Ricky walked towards their limousine.

When they got back to their room they decided to take a nap. Bianca still had several hours before her performance. Ricky had to get back to Los Angeles.

Bianca was so exhausted afterwards she wanted to cry. It was only ten thirty and She felt like her body had shut down completely. She had to schmooze with a few key people and act like she was happy to see them. She desperately wanted to cancel her spa appointment and didn't care if they charged the five hundred dollars to her credit card. She couldn't do it because Mia was coming in town for the day and she did hear Bindi massages and pedicures were incredible.

Bianca interviewed with Becky Stallers from the New York Days last month and she told her the pedicure was for two hours and lasted for two weeks and the massage was fabulous. Bianca told Mia about this, so of course, she felt like she had to experience it, too. She didn't have that much free time so she decided to fly in for the day. Bianca wanted to go to the whirlpool first because after the treatment, they tell you not to wash because the oils need to soak into your skin. Bianca met Mia in the VIP waiting room of the Camel Raw Resort in Sedona.

"I'm so sorry that I'm late," said Mia.

"That is quite all right. If you will go straight to the back, the ladies will give you your robe and slippers."

"Thanks a bunch," said Mia.

"You are quite welcome." She walked to the back.

"This was the best. I really needed this," said Mia.

"I want to lie down. I'm going to call Becky and tell her she was right," said Bianca happily running her fingers through her damp hair.

"I feel like I'm walking on a cloud," said Mia.

"Did you ladies enjoy yourselves?" asked the blonde clerk at the computer.

"Enjoyment is an understatement," said Mia. It was fabulous."

"I second that." Bianca added.

"We're glad you enjoyed yourselves," said another clerk star-struck by Bianca's presence.

"I feel like a million bucks," said Bianca.

"You are worth a million bucks! Literally!" Mia said jokingly reminded Bianca. They laughed.

"The food was great. No one is bothering me, asking me for an autograph or anything," said Bianca.

"I don't want to go back home. I want to stay for another day but I can't," said Mia. "You never have to leave the resort."

"I'm not until tonight!" Bianca said happily.

"Hello, ma'am, your car is here to take you to the airport," said the driver breaking up their fairy-tale feelings.

"Already? I'm coming." Mia frowned. The driver walked back to the limousine. They finished drinking their wine and walked towards the front entrance.

"Thanks for coming to chill out with me, best friend."

"Girl, please. You know you don't have to say this."

"I love you."

"I love you, too. Call me as soon as you get into L.A."

"You'll be on stage."

"I know, leave me a message."

"I'm coming, sir." Mia bent down to tell the limousine driver. He got out of the car.

"Take your time. I'm not in a rush. Do you have bags?"

"No, this is it. This was a day trip." They hugged once more. "I will speak to you later. Have a safe flight."

Mia got in and rolled down the window. "I will." The limousine driver pulled off.

Bianca looked around admiring the beauty of this special place. Thank goodness. This is the first day in months that she had not reached in her purse for an Advil. However, she still had to take five other medications. She couldn't forget.

CHAPTER 31
STRESSED
RICKY

Ricky loved Arizona but had to get the hell out of there. He hated going places when he didn't see people that looked like him. If he could just tour urban cities, he would be satisfied. White people have it made, he thought. They can go anywhere in this country and live because they see similar faces. Well, almost anywhere. Boston was a perfect example. When he saw all of the colleges lined up next to each other, it confirmed his belief that they were lucky. He imagined how it would be if those were all black schools. One big party!

Ricky realized he hadn't spoken to his cousin in a few days.

"What up Scooter?"

"Hey man, what's up?"

"I just woke up. I've been really fatigued lately. I came home and had to take a nap. Well, I smoked a blunt first."

"What else is new? You are always tired."

"So what's up?"

"Actually, I'm still in the studio in New York. Are you back in L.A.?"

"Yeah, I came back early. I was tired. Bianca didn't really need me there for the last day. Mia flew in for their spa day and Bianca is performing for this charity event for celebrities. That in itself is very political so she will be surrounded by lots of key people."

"Really, why is that?"

"It's a long story and I know you're in the studio."

"Yeah, I have to go. I'll be back tomorrow night. Hey, I saw your mom."

"Really, that's cool. How is she?"

"She's fine. She said you never call her."

"Whatever." Ricky was annoyed.

"Call me when you get in."

"I will."

"Later." Ricky clicked the off button, pissed about his mother's comment. The nerve of her to tell him that. She failed to mention that every time they spoke, she asked for money, Ricky thought. It wouldn't be a problem if she were a normal mother. He got tired of giving her five hundred dollars for every phone call. The last time they spoke, she aggravated him so bad he wanted to go through the phone. He told himself he would not call her for six months. She constantly bitched about everything. The last thing he said to her was, *if you don't like your life, change it.* Ricky would tell her to start her life over by getting rid of her loser man. She hung up on him their last conversation. *Good riddance,* he thought to himself. He remembered yelling *fuck you really loud* afterwards. He sat in silence smoking a blunt and drinking Hennessey. She messed up his whole day.

Ricky got up and went to his dresser and got the other joint that was left in his ashtray and lit it. He sat back down on his bed, closed his eyes and took a huge puff. He held it in for a few seconds. He could sit there all night puffing on blunt after blunt trying not to think about how his life was and the mess that he made of it. The phone rang. He heard it but he couldn't move out of his zone. He continued to puff on his blunt. The answering machine came on.

"Hey Ricky, its Delaney. I was trying to catch up with you to see if Bianca was there or if you knew her whereabouts. I called her on the cell and got the machine. Yes, I left a message but that turkey didn't call me back. My mom said you were going on the road with her for part of ...." Ricky interrupted her as he got up in slow motion.

"Hey Delaney." His voice was very monotone and low.

"What's up? How are you doing?"

"Hey Ricky, I'm great. Are you screening your phone calls?"

"No, I was on my way out the door. He lied. "I ran back in because I heard the phone ring. How is the family?"

"They are wonderful," Delaney responded.

"How is Big E?"

"Eric is great. He had a little cold but he's fine. I figured you were on tour with Bianca."

"I was but I left her in Arizona. I had to get out. It was too many white folks!" They both laughed. "I'm kidding. Really, I had to come back early because I was needed in the studio."

"I didn't really want anything. I was just checking in on my big sis."

"She is great. She had a minor little breakout in Spain but she is fine. You know your sister, she blew it into a huge deal. She canceled a show and was freaking out."

"Wow, is she all right?"

"She's fine. The doctor said it was something she ate."

"What did she eat?" asked Delaney.

"I don't know. She was fine in a few days. The swelling went down."

"I don't blame her for getting upset. I would have been upset, too."

"I know you are a Baxter!"

"I'm glad she's okay. How is everything with you?"

"Everything is good. I've been really busy. I'm going back to New York on business. Hopefully Adar and I can hang out. He's never around. I will probably give him a call," said Ricky.

"That's cool. Don't party too much," said Delaney.

"He's so busy we probably won't be able to meet up."

"He barely finds time for his family. Good luck with hooking up with either one of my brothers. My husband and child are here to pick me up so I have to go. They're taking me out to dinner."

Ricky was relieved because the weed had somewhat peaked and he didn't want Delaney to know that he was high.

"Ok, well, I'll tell Bianca to call you if I speak with her first."

"Hold on Ricky, Eric wants to say hello."

Damn, can a brother enjoy his buzz? Eric is cool but these people are fucking up my high! Ricky thought.

"What's up man? How have you been?" Asked Eric.

"I can't complain. Things are going great. I just got in from Arizona with your sister-in-law and I'm on my way to the studio." Ricky said trying to respectfully give Eric a hint.

"I'm not going to keep you, brother man. Handle your business. When are you coming out to visit?"

"I don't know. We'll probably come some time in the fall. My schedule has been really hectic."

"I truly understand," said Eric.

"Can I say hello to Aunty Bianca and Uncle Ricky?" said Bryce.

"Honey, Aunty Bianca is not on the phone. It is just Uncle Ricky." Ricky heard Delaney talking to Bryce in the background.

"Can I say hi to Uncle Ricky?" Bryce whined.

"Ricky, do you have one second to say hello to Bryce?" Asked Eric.

"Sure, put him on the phone." Ricky felt bad because he was high and secretly pissed. He felt like his words were being stretched. Eric passed Bryce the phone.

"Hello Uncle Ricky," said Bryce in his cute little raspy voice.

"Hello little man, how are you?" Ricky tried to talk cheery and faster but the weed wouldn't allow it.

"I'm fine," said Bryce.

"Have you been a good little man?" asked Ricky trying to find the appropriate words to say.

"Yes, I have. Aunty Britney is moving there soon," said Bryce.

"Yes, I know. We are looking forward to her coming," Ricky lied because he was tapped out of words.

"We may come and visit once she gets there," said Delaney in the background. Ricky wanted to hang up the phone.

"Okay Bryce, say bye to Uncle Ricky," said Eric. "He has to go to work."

Thank goodness Ricky thought. He couldn't take it anymore. He was going to explode.

"My daddy said that I have to go now."

"Okay, little man, I hope to see you soon."

"Bye Ricky," yelled Delaney in the background.

"Tell Delaney I said bye." Ricky said faking his interest in the conversation while secretly being excited to terminate the call.

"Okay, take care," said Eric.

"I will." Ricky hung up quickly before they could start another conversation. He jumped up out of bed realizing he had to leave. He slowly searched for his keys. His mind was racing because he had to get to the studio, but his gestures clearly projected a man on cruise control.

A cloud of smoke appeared as soon as Ricky stepped off of the elevator. The smell of weed oversaturated the studio.

"That's what I'm talking about. Can I get a hit?" he asked one of the guys in the corner chilling on the gray leather couch in the corner.

"What's up Ricky?" Jacob walked over to shake his hand.

"What's happening fellas?" Ricky responded while firing up the thick joint passed to him.

"Shhh, the on air monitor is about to come on," said the engineer.

"How are the guys doing?" Ricky asked one of the producers.

"They're doing great but it's going to be a long night," said another producer, as his eyes looked exhausted.

"What else is new? That's why I'm late," said Ricky.

CHAPTER 32
PICK UP
BIANCA

Bianca picked up Britney from the airport four hours later than scheduled because the silly girl missed her flight. This was a bad sign.

"How was your flight?"

"It was okay. I'm really tired, though. Sorry I missed my other flight. I was running around doing some last-minute errands and time got away from me." Britney started coughing. "Excuse me. I've had a sore throat for a while. Anyway, next thing I knew I had an hour to get to the airport and I still had to go home and get my things."

"It's cool. I started to make your butt take a cab but Ricky said that would be messed up. Are you okay?"

"I'm fine. Mommy gave me some Theraflu."

"Are you hungry?"

"No, I picked over some food on the plane. Thanks sis for letting me come and stay with you," Britney said in between coughs. "I really appreciate it."

"No problem." Bianca reached over and patted her on the back. "Are you okay?"

She cleared her throat. "Yeah, I wondered if I was coming down with the flu. I went to the doctor. He ran some tests but I never went back. Daddy said the Doctor called a few times but I never returned his phone call."

"Why?" said Bianca.

"I have been too busy. I kept forgetting. I guess I should have called him," said Britney.

"Do you want to stop and get something to drink?"

"No, I'm fine," said Britney after clearing her throat again.

"Delaney said she is going to come out next month. She and Eric came over to visit yesterday."

"Did they bring Bryce?"

"Yes, of course. He is so cute. He said to Mommy, 'Nana Soupy, do you feel like taking me to the movies?' Mommy said, 'when?' He said, 'when do you think?' 'Right now.'" We cracked up.

"Wow, I still can't believe he is five already. Where did the time go? Delaney called me the other day. She said she thinks she might be pregnant again."

"Yeah, she was telling me," said Britney. She and Eric are so cute together. They look like twins. They both have that same reddish brown hair and the same bone structure."

"I always tell her she should model," said Bianca.

"She always said she should have been a model. She's tall and naturally thin."

"I don't know why she didn't get into modeling," said Britney.

"I don't know either. She says it is too late. She's too old," said Bianca.

"She keeps saying she is going to quit her job."

"I told her to just do it," said Bianca.

"There is this website called *www.myboss.sucks.com*. I told her to post her boss's information on the web." They laughed.

"What is that going to do?"

"It will give her self-satisfaction."

"What is it again?"

"It is this *I Hate My Boss* website. It has funny stories about people's bosses. One girl said she was tired of her boss hitting on everyone in the office. Men and women! A guy said his boss was a micro-manager. He was told he couldn't have anything on his desk that was not related to his job including coffee mugs, books, and his water bottle! It's hilarious. I'll show you the website one day when you're not busy."

Bianca laughed so hard she was hitting the steering wheel while driving. "You are kidding!"

"I'm serious. There was another guy that said his boss was a stinking pig and often smelled like Cheetos Monday thru Wednesday and Corn curls, Thursday and Friday!" They both laughed loud.

"Who would make up such a website?" Bianca sincerely asked.

"People that think their boss sucks! I'm not the least bit mad at them. I wish I could have made it up," said Britney.

"Why, you don't work." They both looked at each other and laughed again. Then, Bianca's cell phone rang.

CHAPTER 33
BROTHERS & SISTERS REACHING OUT
BIANCA

"Hello."

"Hello," said Adar.

"Hello."

"Hello," said Adar again.

"Hello," Bianca raised her voice.

"Hello," said Adar one more time.

"Hello, who's this?"

"It's me, your fine brother."

"Adar, why the heck do you keep saying hello?"

"Because you keep saying hello."

"Well, when I answer my phone, hello is what I say. Da... Anyway, what's up, brother?"

"Nothing, just chilling."

Adar had a cocoa-bean complexion with dark bedroom eyes. He was twenty-eight and finishing his last year of law school at Columbia University in New York.

"I can never reach you at home so I thought I would call you on your cellie. Did Britney get there yet?"

"Yeah, she's right here. I just picked her up. We're in the car on our way home.

"I called the house and Mom said she had missed her flight. I told her I was not surprised. Let me speak to her."

She passed the phone to Britney. "What up brother man?"

"Nothing, I was calling to see if you made it there okay."

"I'm here. I'm tired though."

"I'm sure you are!"

"I can't wait until you take the bar so that I can visit you."

"When is he taking the bar?" asked Bianca.

"In July."

"You are always busy with your life, so I never know what is going on until the last minute. Are you still dating the Chinese chick?"

"Britney, you are so rude." Britney looked at Bianca coyly as she listened for Adar's response.

"What, that wasn't rude," she turned and said.

"Her name is Sandi and she is Japanese and black." Adar said. "She is a good woman. She treats me like a king."

Bianca could hear him and his big mouth. "She's smart, does my grocery shopping and cleans my house."

"That's because she knows you are going to get paid in full."

"She makes tons of money, too. She has been a lawyer for two years."

"Britney, give me the phone. You just got here and you're already starting trouble."

"Okay, okay, I don't want to talk about her anymore. If she makes you happy then that's cool."

"She does make me happy. You all are too judgmental."

"So what else has been happening? When are you coming to visit?"

"I don't know. It will not be until I finish studying. Maybe in a few months." Bianca could still hear his big mouth even though she was behind the wheel driving.

"How is studying coming along?"

"It's coming. I'll be glad when it's over."

"Tell Adar that we're pulling into the garage so call us in the house in a few minutes."

They arrived at Bianca's home. It was smoggy outside. Bianca pressed the button on the remote for the garage door to open, pulled in, and clicked the remote for the garage door to shut. She turned off the ignition and she and Britney got out of the car. The servants carried all six of Britney's Louis Vuitton bags into the house.

"Your room is this way," said Bianca.

They took the elevator up to the third floor. Britney's room had a king-sized bed with brown and black leopard curtains and matching comforter set. The rug was a plush brown and the dressers were crème with brown drawers. There was a full-length mirror in the corner with leopard trim to the left of the balcony that overlooked the south side of Los Angeles.

"Wow, this is beautiful," said Britney.

"I told you I needed to get your room set up. I'm glad you like it."

"Okay, I'm going to lie down now," said Britney. She began to cough again.

"Rocki, can you bring Britney some ice tea?" Bianca asked on the intercom.

"I'm not feeling that well. Maybe I have jet lag from the flight. Thanks Bianca."

"You're quite welcome. Get some rest." Bianca walked out of the room and took the elevator down to her office to do some last-minute paperwork. Upon entering, she hit the play switch that had been built into the wall for the CD player. The jazz classic old school song, "Sorry" by Will Beals began playing in the background.

Bianca's office was a contemporary setting with a large cherry wood desk. She had a floor model television with a VCR and DVD built in. In one corner was a CD collection of over 10,000 CDs, but she probably only paid for about twenty-five of them. In the left corner was an orange Macintosh bubble computer with a printer. Next to that was a black telephone with four phone lines. The fax machine was on top of a glass coffee table next to a small copy machine. She sat down on the charcoal brown leather reclining chair and realized Adar never called back. She wasn't surprised. He probably got preoccupied doing something else. Just then the phone rang.

"What's going on big sis?" asked Armani.

"I just got home from picking up Britney from the airport," said Bianca.

"Oh, what are y'all doing?"

"Nothing, she's sleeping right now."

"Brit is sleeping? I can't believe it."

"Me neither. I was kind of surprised myself. She said she was tired."

"What's up with you?"

"Nothing, just taking a break from studying."

"Oh, when do you take your boards?"

"In six weeks."

"Wow, that's soon! Are you stressed?"

"A little. I just want it to be done. I'm tired of having no life. All I do is work and study. I haven't gotten my hair cut in three weeks."

"I'm sure it's not that bad. You're still a handsome man." Armani was six foot three inches tall with a deep brown complexion, dark eyebrows, a goatee and thin sideburns. He had attended Howard for undergrad and Medical School.

"Oh, I know that. I'm a Baxter. I'm just tired of waking up studying and going to bed with tomorrow's study schedule on my mind."

"Well, it's almost over. How's DC?"

"DC is DC. I have no complaints."

"I just called to say hey and see what was going on with you," said Armani.

"Hey, how is lovely Angie?" asked Bianca.

"She's fine. I'm thinking about asking her to marry me after I pass the boards."

"It is about time. You two have been together for five years."

"It hasn't been quite five years. Don't forget that we broke up for almost three months."

"That doesn't count. She called you during that time damn near everyday," said Bianca in her don't-even-try-it voice.

"She had to make sure no one scooped up this wonderful man!" They both laughed.

"You are your father's child." Bianca laughed.

"Damn right. She knew what she was doing," said Armani with confidence in his voice.

"I think it was both ways.

You probably were calling her just as much."

"You may be right but I still say she knew I was a good catch and she had better get back to DC as quickly as possible."

"Why did you two break up again? I forget."

"She wanted to go back home to North Carolina and work in the courthouse there for the summer. Her father is a judge there. I was not about to engage in a long distance relationship. My needs are heavy duty."

"You mean your ego is heavy duty!" Bianca chuckled. Armani let out an egotistical laugh.

"Did you cheat on her?" asked Bianca.

"I don't call it cheating because technically we weren't going together. Did I mess around with other women while we were broken up? I sure did."

"Did you tell her?" asked Bianca.

"Not right away, because it was none of her damn business. I didn't love the women but they served a purpose! Eventually, we talked about it. She was hurt but she dealt with it. She said she didn't mess with anyone. It worked out okay because I think we missed each other more than anything and of course she came back begging at the end of the summer! She is a great woman and I really don't know what I would do without her."

"That is sweet. I hope you have told her that."

"She knows how I feel."

"Does that mean you have shared how you feel with her?"

"Absolutely. I love my woman and I tell her everyday. Well, not everyday but quite often. I'm not trying to be completely open. Damn sis."

"What time is it?" asked Bianca.

"Ten-thirty my time. I have to go."

"Okay, I'll call you next week."

"Okay," said Armani. Bianca was startled by whimpering sounds through her intercom as she hung up the phone.

CHAPTER 33
PAIN
BIANCA

She got up and turned down her music. She walked slowly to the door and opened it. The whimpering sounds turned into cries of pain. Sharp screams of someone's pain burst through her insides. She realized these screams must be coming from Britney's room, because she had given the staff the night off.

"Oh my God. Help me. Please help me. B-I-A-N-C-A. Please come quick."

Bianca ran out of her office and climbed two steps at a time. Bianca didn't think to take the elevator. She got to Britney's room, opened her door and ran inside. Britney was lying in a fetal position screaming and crying.

"Oh my God, Brit, what's wrong? What is it? Tell me where it hurts."

"My..." she stuttered, in between cries.

"Do you want me to call the ambulance?" Britney nodded her head *no* while crying heavily. Bianca yelled for Rocki but quickly remembered Rocki had left. "Forget it, I'm calling the paramedics." Bianca picked up the phone on the nightstand and dialed 911. She had let her staff leave early because she wanted to bond with her sister. She told the police who she was while breathing heavily. She gave them the necessary information and yelled into the phone for them to hurry. Britney continued to cry in the background. At times, her cries were loud. Bianca hung up the phone and sat on the bed next to Britney consoling her. She didn't know where to touch her for fear she would make her pain worse. Bianca assured her she was going to be okay, then called security to let them know the paramedics would be coming. She hung up before they could ask any questions.

"The paramedics are on their way, Britney. Hang in there, sweetie." Britney began to cough uncontrollably again.

Minutes later the paramedics arrived at the house. She pressed the buzzer to let them in.

"Up here," she yelled.

They ran upstairs with their equipment. They asked Bianca several questions and attempted to ask Britney, but she was in way too much pain to respond.

"Look, just put my sister on the damn stretcher and get her to the hospital as quickly as you can."

"Okay, Miss Baxter."

They put Britney on the stretcher and into the ambulance. Bianca ran downstairs, grabbed her cell phone and new car keys off of the wall, and jumped into her red, two-seater SL55 AMG Mercedes. She was too flustered to figure out how she had misplaced the keys to her black BMW she and Britney had just been in a few hours prior. Stress was kicking in full force. Her heart was racing. Everything happened so fast. Once she got into her car she grabbed her cell phone and called Ricky.

"Meet me at Cedars-Sinai Hospital now. They're taking Britney in the ambulance." Click. She turned her phone off and hung up. She was not quite sure why she turned it off.

Bianca pressed the accelerator to keep up with the paramedics. They pulled into the lot of the hospital. The paramedics went to the right. She had to go to the left to park, and luckily there was a space close by. She parked, jumped out and ran towards the emergency entrance. She soon realized that she forgot to get a ticket from the parking attendant. She thought she heard someone yelling but the welfare of Britney was the only thing she could think of. At the very next moment she was standing at the emergency room front desk, people recognized her, and stared. But right then, she was only Bianca Baxter, Britney's big sister.

"Hello, my sister Britney Baxter was brought in a couple of minutes ago."

"Yes, Miss Baxter, can you fill out these forms please," said the receptionist.

Bianca reached on the counter to grab the clipboard. Her hands were shaking uncontrollably.

"Is she going to be okay?"

"Miss Baxter, I'm not sure. I saw them roll her through the doors. There was a Doctor and two nurses with her."

"Okay." She took the clipboard, sat down and began filling out the form as best she could. Upon its completion she stood up and gave the receptionist the clipboard and paperwork. Ricky was walking in her direction.

"What happened?"

Bianca told Ricky what happened. He started asking lots of questions. She kept telling him that she didn't know anything.

"Ricky, I don't know anything. I told you everything I knew."

Several hours passed. She was a basket case. The doctor finally came out.

CHAPTER 35
WORRIED
BIANCA

"Miss Baxter, hi I'm Doctor Jacob Katz."

"Is my sister going to be okay?"

"Have a seat," said the Doctor.

"I don't want to have a seat."

"I really think you should sit down." Ricky walked towards the chairs and motioned for her to sit down.

"No, I don't want to sit down. I'd rather stand," Bianca said in annoyance. "I'm getting aggravated."

"Okay, that's fine. We have Britney sedated right now. From the urine sample, it looks like Acute Glomerulonephritis."

"What the hell is that?" asked both Ricky and Bianca.

"It is a temporary inflammation of a portion of the kidney that filters waste products from the bloodstream. Disorders of the kidneys range in severity, producing symptoms as mild as temporary loss of appetite to severe tissue deterioration and possible death."

"Possible death," Bianca whispered while she felt her blood pressure slowly rising.

Her mind flashed back to when she picked Britney up from the airport and asked her if she was hungry. She said she had eaten a little bit on the plane but wasn't hungry. Britney had also lost a lot of weight. Bianca ruled out the situation being coincidental. She tuned back to the doctor.

"How in the hell did she get that?"

"There are numerous ways one can have kidney failure. Have you noticed any changes in her diet or behavior?"

"I'm not sure because she just moved here earlier today from Massachusetts. What can I do? Is she going to be alright?"

"She also has a severe yeast infection."

"She complained of a sore throat." Her mind was racing. She started thinking in a negative direction. "Doctor Katz, what does this mean?"

"It could mean a number of things. I would rather not say right now. We'll take a blood test and get the results in a few days."

"What kind of blood test?"

"I don't want to scare you so let me further investigate and let you know. In the meantime we would like to keep Britney here for a few days to monitor her."

"Oh my God, I have to call my parents!"

"I think that would be a good idea."

Bianca looked at the doctor with a concerned look and tried to read his face to determine the severity of the situation. "There is really nothing you can do for her right now. You all should go home and I will give you a call when I know something and the test results are in." Dr. Katz turned to walk away.

"Dr. Katz?" He turned around. "Is there anything else I should know?" Bianca had an eerie feeling in her gut.

"No, Miss Baxter. I have given you all of the information I have thus far. I will call you tomorrow morning."

"Come on honey. He'll call us," said Ricky. Bianca ignored him.

"Can we see my sister?"

"She just went to sleep. Remember, I told you she was in a lot of pain so we had to sedate her?"

"I understand but I want to see her."

"Okay, follow me."

Ricky got up and they both followed the doctor through the double doors past emergency and into Britney's private room.

"I'm sorry but I can only allow the immediate family in the room."

"I'm Bianca Baxter. We both need to go into my sister's room." Bianca surprised himself. Britney was sleeping with her hand on her stomach. She had tubes through her nose and a needle coming out of her arm attached to an IV. Bianca walked over to her and lightly picked up her free hand. She bent down, kissed her on the forehead and whispered to her.

"Britney sweetie, I'm here. I love you. The doctor says you are going to be fine."

Ricky walked over to Bianca and whispered in her ear. "Bianca let her sleep. You don't want to wake her because she is in pain."

"I just want her to know that I'm here for her and I love her."

Ricky turned and looked at Britney lying there on the bed. "I hate hospitals."

"Britney, little sis, you are going to be just fine. The doctor wants us to let you get your rest. He is going to run a few tests but you will be fine."

"She's not in a coma," said Ricky.

"I know but I don't want her to be scared. I think I'm going to stay here. I will call my parents from here."

"Are you sure? There is nothing you can do."

"I know but I want to be here when she wakes up. I don't want her to feel alone. I need you to go to my house and get me some toiletries and a change of clothes. Can you call my assistant and cancel my concert dates and appearances for the next couple of days?"

"Bianca, this is not that serious," Ricky whispered to her.

"Look, this is my sister. Can we go out in the hallway?" They quickly walked out of the room. "I don't feel comfortable leaving her here alone."

"I know, honey, but there is nothing you can do for her now."

"Ricky, please do not argue with me right now. I'm asking you to do me a favor."

"Okay, no problem."

"The keys are in my purse." Bianca turned and walked back to her sister's room where she had left her belongings. Ricky had his own set of keys but his privileges were taken away a long time ago. Ricky followed her.

"Call me on my cell if you hear anything between now and the morning." He kissed her.

"Okay, I will." He left the room. Bianca sat down in a chair next to Britney's bed and looked at her watch. Gosh, it was midnight. She wondered where the time went and realized she needed to call her parents. She laid her head down on the chair and put her feet up on the windowsill. She closed her eyes and said a prayer for her little sister.

CHAPTER 36
MEANING
RICKY

Ricky hated hospitals. The smell made him want to throw up. He hoped Britney was all right. Bianca didn't need any more drama in her life. He knew he had put her through enough. His head felt cloudy. A hundred things were going through his mind. He kept flashing back to that night in the hotel suite with Britney.

He fumbled with Bianca's keys. He turned the alarm off, opened the door and walked inside, then immediately went to the refrigerator. He grabbed a soda and sat down on the couch to gather his thoughts. The phone rang. He didn't feel like getting up to answer it. The ringing stopped. He pulled out his cell phone to call Bianca's assistant Tisha so she could make the necessary changes in Bianca's schedule. Hopefully she would not mess this up as she often did everything else. He then got up and went upstairs to get Bianca some clothes. The private phone rang again. Ricky answered.

"Hello."

"Hello, who is this?" The man was loud.

"Who is this? You called here," said Ricky with a funky attitude.

"This is Joseph Baxter, Bianca Baxter's father."

"Oh, sorry, Mr. Baxter, this is Ricky." He changed his tone to a more polite voice.

"Ricky, do me a favor."

"Sure, Mr. Baxter."

"Don't answer my daughter's damn phone with that attitude again. Do you understand, young man?"

"I'm sorry, sir, I…."

"Never mind," he interjected. "Do you understand?" Joseph asked in a stern voice.

"Yes."

"Okay. Now that we got that straight, put my daughter on the phone."

"She didn't call you?"

"No, she didn't," Joseph said with a question in his voice.

"Mr. Baxter, she's not here." Ricky stumbled with his words because he didn't want to be the one to break the news. *Why didn't Bianca call her parents? She said she was going to call them when I left,* he thought.

"Where is she?"

"She took Britney to the hospital."

"What hospital? What happened?"

Supreme picked up another phone in the house sounding frantic.

"Ricky, what happened? Are they hurt? What...."

"Supreme, he can't answer because you keep talking," said Joseph.

"I'm sorry honey."

"I'm not sure what the problem is." Ricky didn't want to go into details of telling them Bianca had called him saying to rush over to the hospital. "I know it had something to do with her kidneys." Ricky said hesitantly.

"Whose kidneys?" the Baxters asked, simultaneously.

"Britney's kidneys," said Ricky. This time unsure.

"What? What about her kidneys?" They both yelled into the phone.

"I'm really not sure what the problem is, Mr. and Mrs. Baxter."

"What hospital are they at?" asked Supreme.

"Cedars-Sinai Hospital."

"Oh Lord Jesus," said Supreme. "What is the phone number?"

The Baxters' other line clicked.

"Hang up, honey. Maybe it's Bianca."

"Okay."

Supreme immediately hung up the phone. Joseph clicked over to the other line.

"Hello. Hello. Hello." *I should have never told the servants to let me answer the phone,* Ricky thought.

"Mr. Baxter, it's still me, Ricky on the line. I guess the person hung up."

"The phone number is 310 555-2345."

"Thank you, bye."

Mr. Baxter abruptly hung up the phone. "That man can be so rude sometimes. Jerk," Ricky yelled. He dialed Britney's room so that he could warn Bianca of her parents' phone call.

A few days passed. Ricky had to contact Bianca's assistant again because Bianca would not go to any engagements. She wanted to wait on the test results. Britney's condition had gotten worse. Ricky left the studio early. On his way to the hospital, he stopped at the In and Out Burger to get a sandwich to eat on the way. He stopped at Fresh Plate to pick up a healthy dish for Bianca.

CHAPTER 37
CRYING SHAME
BIANCA

Bianca walked out of the room to get some air as she heard the phone ring. It was probably Ricky. She couldn't talk to him at the moment. She had to leave and gather her thoughts. Her poor sister was helpless. Her heart was filled with so much fear. However, she was too scared to cry. She couldn't wait until she was well again so she could tell Britney how she scared everyone to death. She felt like she lived in the hospital. The past few days had felt like months.

While Ricky left the hospital in the morning to go to the studio Bianca decided to turn her cell phone off and take a drive through Beverly Hills to clear her head. They agreed to meet back at the hospital in two hours.

Bianca drove down Robertson slowly looking at all of the restaurants and shops. She turned onto Wilshire and drove for miles bypassing a lot of the red lights. The stress was so overwhelming she didn't have the desire to stop and shop. She eventually got caught at a red light and immediately fell asleep. She was awakened by angry people blowing their horns. She looked at her watch and realized she had been gone for a while and would be fifteen minutes late by the time she arrived back at the hospital.

Bianca and Ricky arrived at the hospital at the same time. Doctor Katz happened to be walking towards them as well.
"Hi Miss Baxter. May I speak with you alone?"
"It's okay. Whatever you have to say to me Ricky can be present." She looked at Ricky.
"No problem. Let's talk in this room." He pointed to an empty private waiting room with soothing colors. It had a pale blue small couch with medal trim and two hard uncomfortable

matching chairs. The floor was a dingy white. There was a 19" television diagonally across from the couch, attached to a wall unit connected to the ceiling. The television was off. Ricky and Bianca sat down on the couch. Doctor Katz pulled the chair closer to them as he sat down.

"Miss Baxter, I'm afraid I have bad news." He paused. "Ma'am, Britney passed away fifteen minutes ago due to complications from AIDS. We did everything we could."

"AIDS. WHAT...?" Bianca's mouth dropped wide open. She had to sit down because she started seeing double. She began to sob uncontrollably. She had an instant migraine. Ricky looked equally as dazed and confused.

She started thinking about herself and her personal situation. Wow, how could God allow two siblings from the same family to experience this? Suddenly her life passed in front of her. She thought about how she didn't have the strength to leave Ricky. Who would want her? She felt she was damaged goods. Because she didn't act like the oldest, now her sister was gone. She couldn't bring herself to say she was.... She went into denial. She came back from denial and freaked out more.

"Miss Baxter, I'm so sorry," said Dr. Katz. I'm going to give you two a few minutes alone. I'll be back." He stood up and slowly walked away.

"Maybe if I had told her about my situation, she would not have made the same dumb mistake," Bianca mumbled. "I have to contact my parents. What will I say? I have to call my brothers, her friends. How do I tell them? You're going to have to call my assistant and tell her to cancel my appointments." Bianca told Ricky. "Who could have done this to her?" She looked at Ricky with innocent eyes. She sobbed loudly and began to tremble. Ricky's eyes watered. Suddenly, Bianca jumped up and ran towards the door.

"I have to see her. This isn't happening. She is not...." She screamed louder. The thought of her dyng next had hit her hard. Living scared with this secret scared her. Ricky ran over to Bianca just as she reached the hallway. He grabbed her and held her tight.

"Bianca, it's going to be all right. Stop crying, honey." He released her from his tight hold so he could look into her eyes.

She was on the outside looking in at herself. She was a mess. She vowed to herself to make some serious decisions in her life. Should she stay with Ricky? She wondered. Should she tell her parents that she has AIDS and Ricky gave it to her? She pondered. She would have her assistant send a check for $100,000 for school supplies to the school that she visited in Africa. She decided she would give Delaney five million dollars to quit her raggedy job. She realized she needed to call Delaney.

"Poor Britney," Bianca cried. Her breaths became swift. She didn't know where her thoughts began and ended. The pain was so severe she couldn't stay in the moment. She had to remove herself from the present.

"Is she okay?" The nurse asked Ricky as she hurried towards them.

Bianca felt fragile and sick to her stomach. She looked down and passed out cold, falling onto the hard frigid floor.

Sharon Braxton is a graduate of Northeastern University, located in
Boston, Massachusetts, and Nations Beauty School in Northern
California. She has been in the entertainment industry for over 10
years and has worked for various entertainment and consumer goods
companies including Turner Broadcasting, Time Warner-
Warner/Elektra/Atlanta Corporation, American Idol, a division of Fox
Entertainment, and Polaroid. She has received awards
for her service and dedication in the music industry.

Sharon currently resides on the West Coast and works in marketing
where she oversees 12 studios in the entertainment industry.

Contact Sharon at: *successfullioness@yahoo.com*